TROPIC DESCENT

A LUKE ANGEL THRILLER

NATE VAN COOPS

Skylighter
Press

ONE
NOSE DIVE

THEY SAY it takes a life of virtue to unlock the gates of Heaven, but a small plane will carry even a tarnished soul to the Bahamas. As substitute paradises went, I knew none better.

Out my pilot-side window stretched a color palette of Caribbean blues: turquoise and sapphire, emerald and aqua.

I'd nearly flunked art class, so I was confident there were more hues to name, but I was just looking forward to splashing in.

Tropic Angel, my 1940s vintage Grumman Mallard, turned several heads as we overflew a fishing trawler motoring its way home to Grand Bahama. My old radial engine flying boat had peeling paint and a battered airframe, but she made up for it in class.

I rocked the wings in a salute to the fishermen before dipping right and turning back on course for North Eleuthera.

Tyson, a young mechanic and trainee pilot on my crew, was leaning against the copilot window looking at his phone.

"I can't decide if I'm gonna have the Rum Runner or a Mojito first at this place." He turned his screen toward me and displayed a cocktail menu from an Eleuthera tiki bar. All the choices came with tiny umbrellas.

"We do have an actual mission to accomplish first. We didn't fly over here exclusively so you can sample drinks."

"A man that works hard like we do deserves a tasty libation at the end of the day." He gestured to the cargo of relief supplies in the back of the plane. "It's only right."

At eighteen, Tyson had barely cracked the legal drinking age of the Bahamas, but apparently that now made him a veteran at manhood in general.

"Let's offload the cargo first. Then we'll see about the Mojitos."

The radio crackled as I climbed through three thousand feet and I fiddled with the squelch.

"Please. Is anybody out there? I need help." The woman was barely audible.

Tyson set his phone down and looked my way.

I adjusted my headset volume. "I heard it too."

The shaky female voice came on the radio again. "My pilot. Please. I can't wake him up."

The controller from Freeport approach came on. "Aircraft calling. Can you say your position?"

"Please . . . Please help." The voice was quieter this time. "I don't know how to fly . . ."

"Oh shit. She for real?" Tyson asked.

"Aircraft calling for help, please say your tail number," Freeport prompted.

But the radio stayed silent.

"November Six One Mike, was that you calling?" The Freeport controller made his request several more times, but with no response.

Tyson and I waited amid the hum of the Mallard's powerful radial engines and listened hard.

"November One Eight Eight Tango Alpha, will you look out your left side, let me know if you see a Cessna 182 at ten o'clock and five miles. Altitude is reading three thousand feet."

I keyed the mic. "Looking now." I pivoted in my seat and scanned left.

"Yo, it's over there," Tyson said and pointed.

The wings of the single-engine Cessna flashed beneath a patchy cumulus cloud in the distance.

"You've got good eyes." I tapped the mic again. "Freeport, we've got that traffic. Looks to be descending."

"Roger, Eight Tango Alpha. That aircraft may be in distress. Advise if you can confirm."

"Altering course," I said. "We'll have a look."

The white-and-red plane was nearly our altitude when we spotted it, but it was losing it fast. The little plane dipped and turned, pitched up and lost airspeed, then gained it again as the nose tilted downward. The engine was running, but it appeared to be underpowered. The plane's twisting course was bringing it closer to the water with each tightening spiral.

"Freeport, I have that Cessna in sight. She's definitely in trouble. Possibly an uncontrolled descent."

"Thank you, Eight Tango Alpha, I'm calling Air-Sea Rescue. Please stay on site, fuel permitting."

I glanced at my fuel gauges. We'd left St. Petersburg, Florida with a heavy load of hurricane relief supplies for the recently battered islands. I'd only taken on partial fuel to compensate for the weight, but we still had reserves.

"We can stay on site for a bit," I replied.

The Cessna headed our way, but it sank lower and lower with nothing but water in every direction.

I keyed the mic again. "Freeport, that plane's going in."

As I said it, the Cessna plunged at a sickening airspeed, like a paper airplane thrown by a child, but it gained lift briefly at the last second, mercifully nosing up just before it hit. The right main wheel and right wing struck first with a terrific splash, geysering water skyward before the plane went tail up, then over, tipping onto its back in the waves.

"Oh shit," Tyson muttered into the intercom. He was on the edge of his seat, peering over the instrument panel as I dipped to keep the airplane in sight.

I radioed again. "Freeport, she's in the water. Now directly below my position."

"Roger, Eight Tango Alpha, we are attempting to contact rescue craft in the area, but they are thirty minutes out at minimum."

"We're in a Grumman flying boat. We'll set down and attempt rescue till they get here."

"Roger, Eight Tango Alpha. Exercise caution. Good luck."

I pulled back on the overhead throttles and idled both engines, losing altitude fast as I dropped *Tropic Angel* into a slip for the last thousand feet. Tyson held on as the bottom dropped out and we plummeted.

"Wind?" I asked.

"Uh, hang on. It's zero-nine-zero," he said, checking the iPad we had mounted to his yoke.

The Mallard might have been a classic, but high-tech she was not. My dash instruments were analog and could have fit in a WWII warbird. But a plane is a plane, and right now we were someone's only hope.

"Fuel's on both, confirming landing gear is up and stowed." I tapped the gear handle behind my seat as I called out the checklist items. "Mixtures rich, props set."

"Ass cheeks, clenched," Tyson said from beside me, and held on to the windowsill.

I brought the Mallard around into the wind and eyed my

suspected touchdown point. The Cessna was still afloat but only barely. The cabin was submerged.

"Yo, someone's in the water," Tyson said, just before I flared the seaplane's nose, pitching for landing. "I think I saw a head."

I kept some power in as the Mallard kissed the water, keeping her on step till we were close enough to the downed plane. I wanted to get close, but not so close that our wake might capsize the already precarious wreck. Finally, I reduced engine power and settled *Tropic Angel* into the waves at a slow plow.

"You getting in there?" Tyson asked.

"Why, are you volunteering?"

Tyson's eyes widened. "I mean, I swim, but I don't like, *swim* swim. Weren't you a G.I. Joe Airborne Ranger or some craziness?"

"Your controls," I grumbled as I unbuckled and slipped out of my seat into the back of the Mallard.

"Oh, yeah, now we're talking." Tyson slid over into the captain's seat.

"Don't you dare hit me with this plane."

"Let me cook. I got this."

Tyson throttled up on the right engine, using differential thrust to turn us left. I'd ditched my flip flops and my phone by the time I reached the hatch. I pulled my shirt off last and snagged a life vest from the aft storage area before popping the hatch door open.

It was perhaps thirty yards to the wreck. There was indeed a body floating in the water. Her face was tilted skyward but she looked to be barely conscious. Behind her, the Cessna was headed to the depths. Only the tail was still afloat.

I planted a foot on the edge of the boarding door, then dove into the iridescent waves.

TWO
SINKER

I SWAM hard for the sinking plane.

Growing up surfing the east coast of Florida had given me confidence in open water, but I had to admit this felt different. I'd spotted sharks the length of Volkswagens in these seas before and they were a lot closer to us than we were to shore. Even so, there was a job to do. I let the life preserver bob beside me as I struck hard for the woman drifting away from the downed plane. By the time I reached her, she was going under. Only her hair was visible on the surface. I caught her three feet beneath the swell and pushed her up into daylight again.

My first priority was getting the life preserver around her neck and keeping her face out of the waves. Once I got it around her, I brushed strands of jet black hair out of her face to check if she was breathing. I couldn't tell, so I tilted her toward me, then pressed my mouth to hers and blew in a couple of quick breaths.

The woman choked immediately, coughed and sputtered reflexively, but her eyes only fluttered.

Could be worse.

Even with the life preserver on, I didn't trust she'd stay face-up without help. Luckily, Tyson had maneuvered *Tropic Angel* closer. He shut down the engines before appearing in the door of the Mallard. He extended the boarding ladder and tossed out a line. I scissor-kicked hard, towing the young woman with me. The moment I reached the line, I looped it through the unconscious woman's life vest and tied it fast.

Tyson started to reel her in.

"Get her aboard!" I shouted.

"How am I gonna do that?"

"Figure it out!"

The empennage of the Cessna 182 disappeared beneath the swell as I swam toward it. I was tempted to dive straight down, but I took a moment to relax my diaphragm, focus on my breathing, and ready myself. My heart rate was already too high for max efficiency in a free dive, but I wasn't about to shortchange myself further. I took my final deep breath, focused my mind, and dove.

Calm.

This would only work if I stayed calm.

It was quiet enough down here.

The plane was inverted and drifting downward, like a flight student practicing a spin in slow motion. The fuel tanks must have had air in them, because something was maintaining partial buoyancy. Per gallon, even avgas is a couple pounds lighter than water. Right now I was grateful for whatever physics was working in my favor.

A short burst of kicking got me to the tail of the plane and I used the structure to climb along by hand from there. The light was already changing, colors vanishing. The fuselage stripes had been red above water but had already darkened here. I reached the pilot side door and found the handle. The door was locked.

The plane slowly rotated as it sank, the underside of the fuselage rolling beneath me. I let it pass and it gave the impression of a huge fish turning belly up. The passenger door was hanging open. Bubbles erupted from it as the plane turned, trapped air escaping in violence toward the surface. The plane's nose cowling had detached in the crash and the torn underside of the engine compartment exposed the shining silver muffler stacks of the exhaust system. The airbox for the carburetor had sheared off completely. This fish had been gutted.

I swam into the open doorway of the flight deck, trying not to focus on the way the plane was pulling me ever downward.

Air bubbles still streamed through holes in the tail cone, but how much air could remain?

The man in the pilot seat bobbed toward me, eyes hazy slits and mouth wide. He was young, or had been. I hurriedly unbuckled his lap and shoulder belt and pulled. He drifted out of his seat, but something arrested his movement. I pulled harder but he was caught. His leg was tangled in the strap of a bag on the copilot side footwell—some type of satchel—the other end of it snagged on the seat height lever.

Air bubbles choked from my mouth and I looked upward. The light was fading. No more orange, no yellow. Green and blue tinted everything. Our sink rate had gradually accelerated.

The void below me yawned black. In parts of the Bahamas we'd be on the ocean floor by now, but not here. I was looking down the shelf of an underwater mountain with a long way left to fall.

The pilot was dead. There was no saving him. But I planted my foot on the door frame for one final pull and something gave way. The young man and the tangled mess of a satchel came together, while the plane sank further into the void.

My lungs burned.

I'd been down for over a minute. I knew that much. Maybe more than two. I kicked. Not thrashing, but with steady determination. Blacking out would do no one any good. I'd drop this guy if I had to. But I was nothing if not stubborn. I fought the overwhelming impulse to breathe and ignored the vise of pressure against my temples. I could last longer. This was a mental struggle first. I could overcome it. The urge to breathe eased some as the light increased, colors brightening as I rose.

Four more kicks, three, two.

I broke the surface with a gasp. I let go of my grisly prize momentarily to get a full breath in my lungs, then snatched at him again, holding his arm to my chest and searching for my plane. I'd drifted, or *Tropic Angel* had. It was probably fifty yards away. Felt farther after what I'd just swum. But I took deep breaths, settled into a rhythm and kicked. My free arm helped.

Tyson's head appeared in the doorway. "You okay, dude?"

I gave a thumbs up. Then I kept swimming.

He tossed the life preserver out again on the line. Same one I'd used on the woman. At least he'd gotten her aboard. By the time I reached the life preserver, I was exhausted. I didn't try to elevate the head of the man I'd recovered. I only grasped the rope and let Tyson pull while I kicked the last few yards.

It's a bear getting into a Mallard without a dock on a good day. Hoisting limp bodies aboard is another kind of difficult altogether. I pushed and lifted, Tyson pulled. I climbed up the ladder beneath the man's dripping corpse. We finally flopped the limp body over the doorsill and I clambered through after.

Inside, we stretched him out on the confined bit of floor near the door and I went through the motions of trying to revive him. Chest compressions first. Tyson had been using a portable aviator's oxygen bottle on the woman—a smart move—and we shifted the mask to the man briefly while I did the chest compressions, but there was nothing to be done. He was gone. Made me wonder if he'd been dead before he hit the water.

Tyson put the oxygen back on the woman and secured the mask to her face.

"Pretty sure she needs a hospital," Tyson said. "She lookin' rough."

I checked the woman over. She was young, maybe early twenties, possibly Bahamian. Black hair. Barefoot now but dressed in patterned medical scrubs. Probably looked better pre-seaweed.

Tyson was looking too. "Girl get a bit of a glow-up, she'd be kinda fine, huh?"

"Did you check her ID?"

"Nah. Couldn't find one," he said.

I picked up my phone and checked our location on Foreflight. I marked the location and took a screenshot for good measure. A Google search brought up the nearest hospital. It was on Sunlit Cay. A town called Hooper's Haven. There was an airstrip. A quick look at the hospital web page showed the place was high-tech. Hooper's Haven wasn't a customs airport, but they'd likely forgive the invasion in an emergency.

Tyson checked the dead man and found a wallet. "ID says this dude's name is Harrison Taylor-Hardy. From West Palm Beach."

"Keep the woman on that oxygen. We'll get her help."

I dripped my way back to the flight deck while Tyson tended to our patient, and I fired up the engines. I slipped my headset back on.

"Welcome to *Tropic Angel*, Air Ambulance," I muttered to myself over the intercom. I glanced back at the dead man on the floor. "Your almost-in-time airline."

THREE
FAMOUS LAST WORDS

THE HANDY THING about flying the islands of the Bahamas—
there are airports aplenty.

With something like seven hundred islands in the country,
getting around means either boats or planes. Or if you're lucky, a
flying boat.

With the bounty of other scenic options available, I'd never
landed at Sunlit Cay before. As the little island came into view
below us, I had my first good look.

It was flat, like most Bahamian cays, roughly the shape of an
acute triangle. Eyeball measurements put it at ten miles long and
maybe five wide. It had the look of an only recently popular
island. New construction was clustered at one end amid a
smattering of older cinder block houses. Trees were plentiful and
the island had craggy ledges along parts of the shoreline. There
were only two settlements connected by one long road. Hooper's
Haven sat at the north end and was sizably larger than the
southern town of Pelican Roost, but if anyone told me the entire
island had more than fifteen hundred residents, I'd eat my flip
flop.

One anomaly on the island was a side road that led to the eastern bluffs where a single enormous house sprawled on perhaps twenty-five acres of cleared land. It had two pools, several athletic courts, and had squeezed in a nine hole golf course and a helipad.

Whoever lived there certainly wasn't in my tax bracket.

The island's airport was located at the north end, a paved strip seventy-five feet wide and thirty-six hundred feet long. The runway ran east to west for the prevailing winds and sat adjacent to a watery cove with a small beach. I approached the airfield from the upwind side.

I'd advised Freeport ATC of my intentions, and the controller promised to call ahead for medical services to meet me at the field. I also explained my plan to continue on for Eleuthera to clear customs after. The controller was nonplussed. Declaring emergency circumstances had granted a lot of latitude.

Tyson strapped himself into an available seat in the back of the Mallard on descent and held on while keeping an eye on our patient.

Passing over the airstrip, I spotted one large hangar and two twin-engine aircraft on tie-down. For rural Bahamian strips, that was busy. An ambulance was making its way along the airport road without lights. Another notable and useful sight was a low wooden fishing pier that jutted out into the cove on the north side of the airfield with a jon boat tied up at one end. A few buoys bobbed in the cove as well.

I keyed the mic and tried my luck with the UNICOM frequency. "Hooper's Haven traffic, this is Grumman Mallard Eight Tango Alpha, overflying the field at eight hundred feet. Do we have the medical vehicle on frequency?"

A warm Bahamian accent greeted me. "Eight Tango Alpha, that ambulance won't hear you, but I have you in sight. I'll direct you when you land."

I spotted the speaker, an old man with a handheld radio standing beside a golf cart near the airfield's self-serve fuel tanks.

I keyed my mic again. "Unless you've got rolling stairs, it would be a lot easier to get our patient out of this plane from the water. You know the depth in that inlet? Can we taxi up close to that dock?"

The old man looked in the direction of the cove. Perhaps no one had ever asked him that before.

"You know, I'll sure go check on that for you." The man climbed aboard the golf cart and zipped away down the taxiway. I circled the field, and a few minutes later I got the reply.

"Plenty deep out here, sir. This pier is sturdy. Bring it on in! If you can't make it all the way up, I'll use the boat."

I reduced power and began my descent.

First order of business was a low pass over the cove and my intended touchdown point outside the inlet, scanning for hazards. The beautiful turquoise water either held no dangers or hid them well. I performed a teardrop turn, aimed into the wind and descended the last hundred feet to the surface, skipping over the light waves till the Mallard settled its belly into the water as gracefully as its namesake. Once *Tropic Angel* sank into a plowing attitude, I applied differential thrust from the right engine and turned for shore.

The island looked bigger from the water's surface.

The pier did too.

Docking a Mallard isn't the most intuitive of procedures. The broad wingspan and lack of water rudders make precision water taxiing a challenge. Best practice often involves tying off to a buoy or anchoring at a distance and then relying upon a boat to get ashore. Getting battered against a pier for any length of time was no one's idea of a good time, but the health of my passenger was in a questionable state and with the already poor condition of the aircraft's paint job, I wasn't opposed to tying off to the pier for a few minutes if we could get there.

It took me a minute to judge the speed of the current and the angle we were drifting at idle, but once I had the feel for it, I brought the Mallard in close to shore. Tyson joined me in the flight deck. "How's it going up here, bossman?"

"I need you in the bow."

"Okay. Tight. I'm on it."

He climbed into the copilot side, swung the second yoke over, then repositioned the rudder pedals on that side, stowing them out of the way. The maneuver opened a small tunnel access. He wriggled under the dash into the tunnel and vanished.

A few moments later, the hatch on the nose sprung open and Tyson emerged. The bow compartment had headset jacks so he donned a headset and gave me a thumbs up. "Plenty deep here. Kinda shallow near that dock though. I don't think you'll make it this heavy."

"Okay. We'll snag that buoy then."

I taxied past the buoy, then turned nose out, just staying clear of the pier with my left wingtip. Then it was a matter of goosing the left throttle enough to counter the current and let the plane weathervane into the offshore wind.

Tyson hooked the buoy with a pole and tied us off to it, then threw out the bow anchor for good measure. He may have been young, but he had good boat sense.

I shut down the engines one at a time, and we made sure we weren't drifting before Tyson squeezed back through the tunnel to the cabin.

The ambulance rolled out to the base of the pier with one woman and one man in the front seats. The driver guy waved to the old man on the dock, then parked the vehicle and got out. They retrieved a spine board from the back, then hustled out to the jon boat. The old man with the radio untied the boat with a practiced hand and had them motoring the distance to us in short order. Airport job or not, I doubted you made it long as an islander if you couldn't handle a boat.

I double-checked the shutdown checklist and climbed out of the flight deck, making my way back through the narrow gap amid our cargo, and reaching the head of our prone passenger. Tyson moved to the woman's feet while I crouched to cradle her head. Sliding one arm under the young woman's shoulders, I propped her head up against my bicep and waited while Tyson got a grip lower down.

"What happens if I accidentally step on this dead guy?"

"Don't."

He used a cautious foot to nudge the legs of the deceased pilot to one side so we'd have space. Then he returned his attention to the woman's plight. But as I removed the oxygen mask from the woman's face, her eyes fluttered open.

"Whoa, hey there." I did my best to smile. "Don't worry. We've got you."

Her gaze was half-lidded, her focus questionable. But her lips parted as she took me in. Even in this half-drowned state, it was hard not to notice how pretty she was.

"A—mericans." The young woman's voice was so soft, I almost couldn't make out the words, "Are we . . . in . . . U.S.?"

"Didn't quite make it that far," I said.

Tyson spoke up. "Hang tough, girl. We're trying to save you. I'm Tyson. You can 'at me' later."

I rolled my eyes. "Let's focus, Ty."

Concerned voices called from the boat. Tyson gave me a nod and started to lift. I kept the young woman propped against me and rose. Her head rocked against my chest.

"Maybe we want to pivot her around and put her out head first," Tyson said, reaching the rear of the aircraft where we had more space. "We're kinda jammed up."

I let him back up while I swung toward the door. The paramedics were waiting in the jon boat with open arms and the spine board. They propped the board on the edge of the boarding door, but it was too long to make it all the way inside without hitting the coat closet.

The woman was barely coherent.

"I'm going to set you on that, okay?" I repositioned myself so I was holding the woman entirely in my arms and Tyson took a firm grip on the end of the spine board.

The woman was relaxed as I eased her toward the board, but when she looked out the boarding door to the waiting boat, and the island beyond, her body stiffened.

"NO. No, no. Not here!" She jerked in my arms and let out a scream. The next moment she went limp in my arms again.

FOUR
NEAR MISS

TYSON and I stood on the pier and watched the paramedics load the body of the dead pilot into the back of the ambulance. The young woman we'd rescued was on the right side of the vehicle, already back on oxygen, but still unconscious. The two paramedics monitored her vitals, and before they left, the female paramedic gave me a reassuring smile. "Don't worry, we'll take good care of her."

The door shut and the crew was lost to view.

We'd flown her to safety, but I was still waiting for the feeling of accomplishment.

"Let loose like a banshee, didn't she?" The comment came from the old Bahamian man with the golf cart who I'd nearly forgotten was there.

He walked up beside us as we watched the ambulance drive away.

"Girl was scared as shit of something," Tyson said. "What set her off like that?"

"You ask me to go to the doctor, I'm the same way," the old

man said. "Shots?" He shivered. "No thank you. Or maybe she's got family in the Roost."

"The south island village?" I asked.

"Superstitious bunch down there. Hate all this new medical whatnot on the north side."

"How long have you been here?"

"Not long. I'm from the Abacos, mind you, but over near Great Guana. I only moved here last year to manage this airport. I'm Basil. You two must be Americans."

"Saint Pete," Tyson said, with an air of pride.

I shook the man's hand. "Appreciate your help today, Basil. I'd take some more if you don't mind boating us back out."

"For that old beauty? You betcha. Been years since I've seen a Mallard. They used to fly into Bimini in those. That one airline, can't recall the name."

I did remember.

"Shame they went under. Danger of flying old planes, I guess." He shrugged, as though that was all that could be said about it.

The three of us climbed aboard the jon boat again and he ferried us back to *Tropic Angel*.

Basil rested both hands on the gunnels of the boat as he waited for Tyson to board the ladder. "You two really did that young girl a great service today. True heroes. I'd best know your names."

"He's Tyson and I'm Luke," I replied.

"Good to know you, Luke." He shook my hand. "Anytime you come back to Sunlit Cay, I bet you'll be real welcome."

I had *Tropic Angel* plowing into the wind fifteen minutes later. Caribbean blue slid beneath us and we escaped the pull of the

water with our shadow dancing off the surface below. Tyson was
back in the copilot's seat and I let him take the controls once we'd
cleared a few hundred feet and I'd reset the flaps. He had a
private pilot's license so far and was building hours in whatever
he could get time in. Logging time in a Grumman Mallard was
rare for any pilot so his logbook already had more highlights than
most.

North Eleuthera was a short hop from Hooper's Haven and
by the time we reached a cruising altitude we were ready to
descend again. Our cargo was a slew of relief items including a
generator and a lot of first-aid and construction supplies.
Eleuthera had been hit hard two weeks prior by an early season
hurricane and was still recovering. Tyson's grandmother, Maddie
Coleman-Martin, sat on the board of Sunshine Relief Services
out of St. Pete and had insisted her grandson get his hands dirty
helping. It was his first trip to the Bahamas by air.

"This is the life, man," he said looking out the window.
"We're like modern cowboys, huh? Rescuing damsels in distress,
rolling into town with supplies." He handed me his phone.
"Here. Get a shot of me flying this thing for my reels." He
adjusted his shades.

"I doubt Maddie sent you on this trip to increase your social
media following." I snapped the photo for him anyway, then
attempted to hand the phone back.

"You gotta do it vertical."

I took another shot of his cheesing grin, then flipped back
to the first to compare. I went too far and saw his previous
photo.

"Wait, you took a picture of the dead guy?"

Tyson shrugged. "I'm not gonna post that, obviously. But I
never seen a dead guy before."

"I'm deleting this. You better not have taken pictures of the
girl."

"Naw, that seemed kinda cringe, cause her shirt was all soggy and whatever."

"But the photo of the dead guy you didn't think was *cringe?*"

"I don't know. Not like he minds."

"This job you want?" I pointed to the seat I was in. "Captain of the aircraft? It's all based around trust. Passengers put their faith in you. They have to be able to trust your judgment."

"Even the dead ones?"

"Dead Guy's got a family somewhere. Show them respect too."

"Yeah, all right. I hear you."

I handed him back the phone.

The runway was in sight now.

"My controls. You get to pump the landing gear out. We're going to test the emergency system."

Tyson grumbled but turned around and got to pumping using the hydraulic handle behind his seat. *Tropic Angel's* landing gear slowly extended from the side of the fuselage in a tricycle configuration. It was more modern than that of the Goose or Widgeon, but modern was a relative term when discussing anything from the late 1940s. I entered the downwind for Runway 7 and made my radio call. North Eleuthera, like many fields in the islands, was a non-towered airport and not especially busy.

Possibly the nicest part of flying the Bahamas as a general aviation pilot was the laid-back vibe of the atmosphere. Despite being one of the most beautiful places in the world to fly, only a select few managed it regularly.

Today we were some of the lucky few.

I turned the base leg over the gorgeous Caribbean water, and was eyeing the final approach when I spotted the jet streaking in toward the runway from my right. It was on a collision course.

I double-checked the frequency I was on. Had I missed a radio call?

I made another. "North Eleuthera traffic, Mallard Eight Tango Alpha is base to final for runway seven, North Eleuthera."

But the corporate jet paid no mind. The call finally came. "Embraer is straight-in final runway seven North Eleuthera, number one." The female voice gave no hint of apology.

The Embraer sank lower, skimming along at four hundred feet and cutting me off without slowing.

"The hell is this chick doing?" I said and added power to climb and avoid them.

I cut across to the upwind and flew the pattern again while the jet landed, taking its time turning around at the end of the runway and slowly back-taxiing to the ramp.

"Guess they think they own the place," Tyson said.

I remade my radio calls on base and final. This time no one was around to cut me off.

Tropic Angel's engines purred evenly on their way in before I cut them nearly to idle and held the plane off the runway. This runway was a generous six thousand feet long and we touched down and rolled out before even reaching the midpoint. A little differential thrust and leisurely braking had us turning left to the FBO and customs building. But we were late to the party. The Embraer Phenom 300 had opened its door and was surrounded by what might be described as a circus. Judging by the cameras, the crowd was full of either professional photographers or high-budget influencers. Someone had laid out an actual red carpet.

"We sharing the ramp with a president or something?" I muttered.

Several security guards emerged from the plane first, kept the crowd back, and then made space for the woman who appeared next. She was dressed in black jeans and a black leather jacket despite the balmy summer heat. She looked young, maybe mid-twenties with a short haircut that involved lines trimmed into it. She waved to the crowd.

"Oh damn. I know who that is!" Tyson declared. "That's E. Z. Breeze."

"Easy Breeze? What is she, an air freshener?" I turned *Tropic Angel* toward an open tie-down spot at the other side of the ramp.

"E. Z. Breeze is her gamer handle," Tyson explained. "Her company made Void Nebula. I know you had to hear of that game."

"Wait, E. Z. Breeze is whatsherface, the tech prodigy?" I shut down the Mallard's engines.

"Mali Solomon," Tyson said. "Yeah. That's her real name. You recognize her now?"

I could admit that even with the limited time I spent on the Internet news, she'd wandered across my awareness more than once.

The young woman was now shaking hands and posing for selfies.

She glanced our way and for a moment our eyes met through the windscreen. She lifted her chin and gave me a head nod. Then she was immediately roped back into another photo op.

Tyson held his phone up and took a picture too.

"This one is definitely going in my reels."

FIVE

DELIVERED

THE WOMAN who processed my customs forms was distracted. She handed back the Bahamas cruising permit, but forgot to give back my passport. She was busy looking out the window at the chaos.

"Big day around here," I said, and pointed to my passport. "You done with that?"

She still hadn't met my eye. "You know she donated three hundred thousand dollars to the Eleuthera cleanup. That's what my sister said."

"Kind of her."

"She's from here, too. Well, from Sunlit anyway. That's where she grew up."

"Over at Hooper's Haven?" I jerked a thumb in the direction we'd just flown in from.

"Yeah. She's got that big mansion over there now. But she built the hospital for the island too. The one all the rich people fly into."

"Is she involved in the medical field somehow? I thought she was a gamer."

She shrugged. "I guess it's related? She's so hot." She said the last bit with a schoolgirl sigh.

"Very attractive," I agreed. "Can I get that back?" I pointed to the passport more aggressively.

"Oh, yeah. Sure." She finally handed it over. "Welcome to Eleuthera."

I walked back out to the ramp and handed Tyson his passport. He'd been joined by Kadisha Jackson, our contact with the local Methodist Church who was distributing our supplies. She wore a yellow Methodist camp T-shirt with paint smears on it and jean shorts.

"Luke, good to see you. I've only got Zeke in the truck today, so it's just us unloading."

Zeke was a wire-haired terrier mutt sitting in the passenger seat of the old truck she'd pulled onto the ramp. His wagging tail was visible from there.

At Kadisha's suggestion, I backed the truck up to the Mallard myself, getting several licks in the face from Zeke in the process.

Tyson directed me with hand signals from the plane's boarding door.

"Maybe we can recruit some of their lot," Kadisha said as I climbed back out of the truck cab. She gestured to the group around the Embraer. If Mali Solomon was getting tired of donating selfies, it didn't show.

"Let's just get to it," I said. I climbed up into the truck bed via the rear tire.

Tyson started handing out supplies to me in the back of the truck. We'd both already worked up a sweat by the time we managed to get the heavy generator squeezed out the door. Tyson had to climb out the emergency exit and come around to help Kadisha and me ease it down. Even so, I had an inkling I'd be paying for the maneuver with my lower back come morning.

In the end, we were sore but smiling. Kadisha surveyed the

fully loaded truck and gave me a satisfied nod. I pulled the truck away from the Mallard a dozen yards for her.

Tyson climbed back into the Mallard for a final sweep of the cargo area and hopped back out with a satchel dangling from one arm. "Is this a donation item too?"

"Oh shoot, that's not ours," I said. He handed over the still-damp canvas satchel. "That came out of the 182."

"Oops," Tyson said. "It belong to that unconscious chick?"

"Who?" Kadisha asked.

While Tyson regaled Kadisha with the tale of our unplanned water landing, I opened the satchel and took a look inside. It was stuffed with several royal blue file folders with maybe a dozen sheets of paper in each. Some of the blue dye from the folders had stained the paper. Another set of files were in a plastic sleeve and had fared better. It was all too soggy to try to read without damaging it though. I fished in a few of the other pockets and only came up with some pens and a thumb drive. I unzipped the last pocket and discovered a passport. It was from the US and showed the woman we'd saved from the wreck. The passport had her name as Fabienne Thompson. She'd no doubt be missing it.

Damn.

I stuffed it back in the satchel.

Kadisha picked up Zeke and the dog wriggled happily in her arms, aiming a few licks at her chin.

"You two have had quite the day. You want to swing by the community hall? They're serving dinner. Probably burgers and hotdogs, but it'll be warm. Maybe I could find us some dessert at my place after."

"Luke promised me Rum Runners," Tyson said.

"You promised yourself that," I countered. "But I think your inaugural Bahamas drinking session is going to have to wait. Unfortunately, we need to head back to Sunlit Cay tonight and return this satchel."

"Oh no," Kadisha said. "Really?"

"What on earth for?" Tyson added.

I explained about the passport in the satchel.

Tyson frowned. "Not like she knows about it. You could yeet that whole thing back in the ocean right now and nobody gonna know."

"I'd know."

"But, duuude. We on island time now. Supposed to be doing island things, like looking at island girls and getting drinks with little umbrellas in 'em."

"I'm sure they have girls on Sunlit. They've heard of piña coladas over there too. And it'll make for a shorter flight home tomorrow. Besides, what's the primary duty of a pilot?"

Tyson looked skyward and answered with his best bored teenager voice. "Get your passengers home safely."

"Correct. And how do we expect her to get home safely without this?" I held up the passport.

"She won't."

"So duty calls."

Kadisha gave a nod of affirmation, but I detected a hint of disappointment in her expression.

"We'll hit you up for that grill-out next time," I said.

"All right, make sure you do that." Kadisha hoisted Zeke higher under one arm and started back toward the truck. The little dog's flapping tail reminded me of a propeller, scooting her along.

"Dude, you and all your 'pilot's duty' stuff is wasting your opportunities out here," Tyson said, keeping his voice low and gesturing to the retreating Kadisha.

"What are you talking about?"

Tyson jerked his head toward the truck. "You think a sister like her doesn't have half a dozen guys she coulda sent to help with this? She came by herself and kept her lipstick fresh."

"She's a nice lady from the church. Where is your mind?"

We headed back to the plane. "All I'm saying, she looking right at you hard when she said she gonna give you dessert later at her place. I don't think she was only thinking church lady thoughts."

I shook my head and did a walk-around of the plane. As I flicked a dead wasp off the bow of the aircraft, a car pulled up behind me. Mali Solomon rolled down the rear window of the Town Car and smiled at me. "Hey, man. I like that plane. Want to sell it?"

"Sorry. Off the market."

"You name the price, I can pay it." Up close, she looked even younger, and twice as brash. Her eyes flashed with a vague mischief.

"I'm sure you could."

"I saw you with that lady from that Methodist church group. You're helping our islands. Good for you."

"Just the delivery boy. Credit goes to the donors."

"That's fine. I'll accept. Since you insist."

I furrowed my brow.

She grinned. "You're that flight from Sunshine Relief over in St. Pete, right?"

"Yeah."

"Had a good talk with your girl Diana over there that runs the show. Told her to send whatever she could and put your flight costs on my tab for this trip."

"Ah. Well, thanks then."

"Another storm's coming later this week, they say. Curse of living in paradise. Seems like we'll keep you busy. But I've got a thing tomorrow night at my pad on Sunlit, pre-stormy weather, celebrating all our relief donors. You should come. I'll put you on the list."

"Not necessary. Especially since you're the one covering my costs. Hardly heroic on my part."

"I'll put you on the list anyway. You should change your mind. It'll give Diana and Sunshine Relief some free press. I've got a reporter from Miami going to give all the charities some love in the news. Plus I want another chance to talk you into selling me that sweet ride. What's your name, man?"

"Luke Angel."

"Angel. Cool. See you tomorrow, Luke Angel."

The window went back up without me needing to reply.

I watched the car roll off the ramp and out into the road. A security vehicle trailed it. Mali Solomon was taking the circus with her.

Young, wealthy, generous. Seemed like Mali Solomon had it all.

One last photographer was on his way toward his car on foot, but before reaching it, he turned and raised his camera and snapped a photo of me and *Tropic Angel*. Almost as an afterthought. He checked his camera display and left. Didn't bother to wave. I wondered what he'd do with the photo.

At least it wasn't a selfie.

SIX

SUNLIT

I WAS STILL VAGUELY DAMP when we landed back in Sunlit Cay, my skin tacky with Caribbean salt.

The cove to the north of the Hooper's Haven airfield still looked calm and inviting, but I used the actual runway this time. The sun was headed toward the horizon and despite a day of stunning ocean views, Tyson and I were both ready to appreciate them from the ground for a change.

The steady thrumming from the Mallard's twin radial engines pulsed between my ears even after I'd shut them down. I'd worn a noise-canceling headset most of the day, but there is only so much modern technology can do when faced with 1940s raw horsepower.

"Still can't believe you turned down an invite for us to hang with E.Z. Breeze at her *mansion*," Tyson moaned. "You know how legit that would be?"

"Hard to attend if we're gone."

"So why be gone? Maybe we develop mechanical trouble and stay another night. Who's going to know?"

"Your boss," I said, rubbing my hand over my hair and finding yet more salt.

"My boss needs to learn to smell the petunias sometimes," Tyson said. "Bet that party will be lit."

There was no sign of Basil and his golf cart this time, so Tyson and I shouldered our overnight bags and hoofed it the short distance down the service road to a stretch of buildings that seemed promising. I lugged the satchel I'd rescued as well.

Lively steel drum music drifted from a waterside establishment that neighbored the airport property. As we approached, I recognized the motif as that of a salvage operation. A bright sign hung above a swinging gate in a picket fence that read "THE BONEYARD" and several salvaged vehicle wrecks decorated what could be called the lawn of the place. It may have once been a house, but part of the structure now consisted of the bow of a boat, while another section of the building was constructed using a modified fuselage from a Douglas DC-3. It was eclectic but inviting.

The Boneyard's bar and restaurant sat adjacent to a small motel called The Windy Palms, and I diverted Tyson from his beeline for the alcohol long enough to maneuver him through the door of the motel lobby. A thin young man with a crooked tie sat reading a book on poker behind the counter. He observed us over the rim of his thick-framed glasses as we barged in. He pushed the glasses to the bridge of his nose and gave us a grimace that might have been his attempt at a smile. "You guys have a reservation?"

"No reservation," I said. "What have you got left?"

"Well, you're not going to get a water view, I'll tell you that." The young man tapped a few keys on the computer keyboard.

"As long as rooms still come with beds, we'll be fine."

"I've got one left with two queen beds on the second floor. But it's down by the bar so it's kind of loud."

"That's okay 'cause we gonna be the ones gettin' loud," Tyson said.

I pulled my ID and credit card from my wallet. "Maybe he will be. Can we get to the hospital along that road?" I pointed out the window.

"The Solomon Center? Sure. Go to the stop sign and hook a left, you can't miss it. Biggest building on the island."

"While you go do that, I'mma hit up this scene over here." Tyson pointed with both thumbs and a dipped shoulder toward the bar, like he was going to samba his way out the door. "It's after five, bossman. I'm off the clock for some Tyson time."

"You'd better pace yourself." I pulled a twenty from my wallet and handed it to him. "Get some food in you before you do too much damage."

"Now *that* I can do." He took the twenty and shot me with his forefinger.

"Give me your bag," I said, trading him a room keycard for it. "I'll make a quick stop up at this medical clinic and meet you back at the restaurant."

"All right. I'll scope out all the ladies for us. See who the lucky ones are going to be to hang with us tonight."

The guy behind the counter watched Tyson leave out the side door, then turned back to me. "Don't worry. They water the drinks down a lot for the tourists over there."

"You're really working hard to sell this place," I said.

The guy shrugged. "Natural salesman, I guess."

I couldn't tell if he had missed the sarcasm in my voice or if he was giving it back to me so deadpan that I was missing his. He just stared at me another long moment and went back to his book.

I walked away with the note to myself to never play poker with him.

I pit-stopped in the room for a quick shower and change of clothes. The shower was small but the water pressure was good.

I'd only brought one other outfit, not expecting to be doing so much swimming in mine on my way in, so I donned the worn-in khakis and a linen button-down I'd planned for the next day.

I rolled my sleeves up and cruised out of the motel with the old satchel over my shoulder and my sunglasses on. The sun was setting in a fiery display to the west, tinting everything a tangerine orange as I walked.

Like in most Bahamian villages, it was a level walk about town with only a slight uphill as I turned at the corner fruit market and made my way toward the Solomon Center. I had my first good look at the place walking up, and it was easy to tell the builders had spared no expense. The roundabout out front featured lush landscaping and a custom mosaic fountain. The ambulance I'd seen earlier was parked to one side. Even that was shiny. I walked through double sliding doors into a briskly air conditioned lobby and was immediately greeted by a cheerful receptionist. He was perhaps twenty-five with a bright white smile that he unleashed immediately. "How can I help you, sir?"

I told him what I was after and his brow furrowed in concentration as he listened.

"Yes, sir. A woman was brought in earlier today. I don't know her condition personally, but I'll let her doctor know you are here."

He picked up a phone and called a nursing station elsewhere in the building.

After a brief chat, he beamed his bright smile at me again. "Good news, sir. Someone will be down to collect you shortly."

I wandered over to a wall display while I waited. A plaque showed the date of the building's dedication with a photo of what I assumed were doctors and staff, and front and center of the shot was Mali Solomon. I was surprised to learn, however, that the hospital name of Solomon wasn't named for her, but rather her mother, Ruth Solomon. As I was reading, the lobby doors opened again and an official-looking man in uniform strode in. The red stripe across his peaked cap matched one running the length of each of his navy trouser legs. He was greeted with the same cheery enthusiasm by the receptionist.

As they turned toward me, I picked up on the conversation.

"I understand, sir. This gentleman is inquiring after her as well. He is the one who rescued her from the plane. If you'd like to wait here, her doctor will be down quite soon to speak with you both."

The uniformed officer met my eye and walked over.

"Hello, sir. I'm Constable Swain from the Royal Bahamas Police. You're the one who performed the rescue." He extended a hand.

"Luke Angel," I said.

His handshake was firm. I put him in his late-fifties, some distinguished gray showing at his temples. He took off his cap and tucked it under one arm. "You came in the flying boat. Beautiful plane."

"Can't hide that thing anywhere."

"It's a small island. Hard to miss such an arrival." He sized me up, his eyes lingering briefly on the satchel. "You're here to check on the woman?"

"You have an update?"

"Yes. Sadly, I heard that the gentleman you brought in didn't survive, as you may be aware. The doctors said there was nothing they could do."

"He was under water for a long time, but it sounded like he might've had trouble even before going down."

I explained about the woman's distress call.

"I've left a message with the Air Accident Investigation Division. They'll do their best to locate the aircraft and see if there were other factors to consider in the fatality. I'd appreciate any and all cooperation you can give them."

"Of course."

"Did you have any contact with the woman you rescued prior to the accident? Ever met her before?"

"Not before hearing her on the radio. I did find something of hers though."

I was about to address the issue of the satchel I'd found, but at that moment the hallway doors opened and a doctor emerged. She had a harried look to her, common to busy medical professionals, but she greeted us cordially.

"You've come for the test results, Constable."

"If you have them. I understand if you need more time."

The doctor looked me over briefly, then turned back to the constable and shook her head. "It was quite definite. In addition to several internal injuries, possibly sustained in the incident, the young man had elevated carboxyhemoglobin levels indicative of carbon monoxide poisoning. The young woman has likewise been treated for carbon monoxide exposure."

"A mechanical accident then," Swain said.

"Will she survive?" I asked.

"Her other injuries don't appear life-threatening at the moment." She addressed me for the first time. "I'm Kathleen Ryan. You must be the rescue pilot."

"Right place at the right time."

"Your heroics are still commendable."

"Were you able to make a positive identification of the woman yet?" the constable asked.

"She had no identification on her," the doctor replied, "but I suspect she'll be awake soon."

"I may be able to help with that," I said. I dug in the satchel at my hip and came up with the passport. "This was in the plane. Didn't find it until after I'd dropped her off. Might clear up a few things."

The constable took the waterlogged passport and opened it.

When he reached the photo page, his brow furrowed. "This is who you pulled from the water?"

"You know her?"

"A woman matching her description was reported to me just this afternoon in a matter of some concern. Been causing some trouble on the island."

He turned to Dr. Ryan. "If this is your patient, I'd like to speak to her when she's awake. I have a few questions for her."

The doctor took the passport for a closer look at the photo. "We can check on her together," she said. "I'm due to make my rounds."

"That won't be necessary, Kathleen," a voice said. A man came walking through the swinging doors, shrugging into a white medical coat. Doctor Ryan turned and her eyes widened slightly.

"Dr. Marcus. I didn't know you were coming in this evening."

Marcus was maybe sixty, but rail thin, having avoided the spreading gut of middle age. He had a pleasant face I recognized from several of the photos on the dedication wall, but his cheeks were vaguely gaunt, as though someone ought to have offered him a sandwich and a good night's sleep more often over the years. His walk was still brisk and purposeful and he greeted Constable Swain with a nod, evidently already acquainted.

Doctor Ryan gave me a brief introduction. "This is the pilot who rescued the young woman we have on C."

"Has she spoken to anyone yet?"

"No. She revived briefly under oxygen but is still resting."

"Good." He studied me. "Typically we only allow family on the recovery floor, but since she owes you her life, I think we shall make an exception."

"Don't break any rules on my account."

"Dr. Marcus is the director of the center in addition to being its chief surgeon," Dr. Ryan said, handing me back the passport she'd been holding. "So the rules are his to bend."

I stuffed the passport back in the satchel. "I'm lucky to know the right people then."

"Leave them with me, Kathleen," Dr. Marcus said. "I know you're busy tonight."

Dr. Ryan backed up a step and invited us ahead of her.

Dr. Marcus scanned a keycard to open the doors again and led the way down the corridor. He seemed in his element. The place wasn't overly busy but looked well-staffed. Everyone greeted him as we passed.

"The dedication plaque called this place a transplant center," I said, still trying to get a read on the man. "That's your specialty?"

Constable Swain intercepted the question. "Dr. Marcus is the preeminent surgeon of the islands for organ transplants, with a splendid reputation."

"With a video game developer as a benefactor? Has to be a story there." We entered an elevator for a brief ride up. The interior was a mosaic of mirrored glass in various colored tints.

Swain continued his explanation. "Dr. Marcus saved the life of Mrs. Ruth Solomon many years ago and has since received the gratitude of her daughter, Ms. Mali Solomon. She has been most generous to our island. She has also been instrumental in its cutting-edge technology."

"You can trust I'd have never dreamed this decor up," Dr. Marcus said, indicating the modern styling of the elevator.

When the elevator doors opened on the second floor, we turned left and wended our way down short hallways before reaching the last room adjacent to the stairwell. Marcus consulted an iPad and read what I assumed was a treatment chart. "It's possible our patient's speech might be unfocused or disoriented," he said. "I wouldn't expect too much of her yet."

Constable Swain nodded. But I noticed he had his hand resting on his gun.

When Dr. Marcus opened the recovery room door, he immediately paused, blocking the path. When he finally stepped forward again, it was easy to see his concern. The hospital bed was empty.

He walked to the ensuite bathroom and poked his head in, but there was no one there.

A window at the far side of the room stood open, the curtains parted.

While Dr. Marcus began questioning the nursing staff in the hall, I walked over and observed the roof of the adjacent ambulance parking structure just out the window. Several footprints from two bare feet were still evident in the dust on the otherwise shiny metal roof.

Constable Swain looked out the window with me and swore.

Fabienne Thompson had flown the coop.

SEVEN
BEST LAID PLANS

THE SOLOMON CENTER was in a state of confusion for no short amount of time as the nursing staff and administrators scrambled to ascertain who had last seen their patient. Constable Swain stormed to the elevator. In the chaos, I was largely forgotten. My phone rang while I was watching the hullabaloo so I answered it.

"Hola."

My shop manager, Reese, was on the other end.

"Having some fun on Eleuthera?" she asked. "Loud there."

I stepped into the nearby stairwell to get away from the chaos. "Got a change of scenery, actually." I tromped down the stairs and found my way to the lower corridor hoping to preserve the phone reception. "I'm on Sunlit Cay."

It took several minutes of explaining to catch her up to speed.

"Good hell," she said. "You've been busy. You still able to get home in the morning?"

"That's the plan. There's a chance they may need me around here for follow up, but I'm still planning to pick up Murphy tomorrow. Probably after lunch."

"No rush. Murph and I are getting on fine." My dog barked in the background. "He says hi."

"Give him an extra belly scratch from me."

"You have an eye on the weather?" she asked. "Heard that next tropical storm is picking up speed toward you."

"I'll check the radar again in the morning, but last I heard it wasn't supposed to affect us for another day or two."

"Might want to consult a briefer. I heard the track is shifting."

I made it back to the lobby of the hospital and wandered over to the reception desk. "Excuse me. If that constable comes looking for me, will you tell him I'm over at The Boneyard bar by the motel?"

"Of course, sir," the man beamed. "Enjoy your stay on Sunlit Cay, sir."

"Geez. Extra friendly over there, huh?" Reese said in my ear.

I walked out the automatic doors back to the fading twilight. "They haven't figured out I'm a ne'er do well yet."

"Tyson behaving?"

"I'm about to find out. He's probably finished a bucket-sized Mojito by now so I may be scraping him off the floor later."

"His young liver is in for a shock. Have fun with that. I'll catch you tomorrow."

"Hasta mañana."

The call ended but I had a smile on my face. The smile faded slightly when I shifted the weight of the satchel at my hip to get through the gate of The Boneyard's picket fence. The pull of the satchel somehow felt stronger than just gravity. I looked back down the dark street. Somewhere on this island was a young woman so frightened that she went out a hospital window and didn't even use the stairs. What the hell was she running from? Then I remembered the constable's hand on his gun entering the room. Or had he been the one who was scared?

Just who was it that I'd fished out of the water today?

The interior of The Boneyard was just as eclectically decorated as the exterior, with bric-a-brac and carefully curated junk pinned to every available bit of wall space. Jimmy Buffet crooned "Changes in Latitude" from overhead speakers. The long wooden bar looped around in a U shape and I found Tyson at one end, a tall and mostly empty cocktail glass at his fingertips. He had collected two tiny umbrellas so far and was busy chatting up a cute bartender in a crop top.

He spotted me coming and waved me over. A plate of crumbs sat in front of him with only a few straggler French fries and a smear of ketchup as evidence.

"Dude, you gotta try the conch fritters in this place," he said, adding a chef's kiss gesture. "On God, it's the best thing I ever ate in my life."

"Sign me up. But let's get a real table."

Tyson turned to the bartender. "This the dude right here I was telling you about. Diving in oceans, saving people. Dude's gnarly."

The bartender gave me a once over. "Kinda hot, too."

Tyson screwed up his face. "I mean, if you like old dudes. He ain't really all that."

The girl laughed. "I'll bring you over that extra order of conch fritters." She gestured to me. "You want a drink, handsome?"

"A Kalik would be fine."

Tyson slid off his stool and headed to a table with me. "I'm tipping that chick fives on drinks for an hour and I don't get called handsome? You been here two minutes."

"Don't worry, she's all yours," I said. "Just play it cool."

"I was born cool."

We slid into a booth at the side of the bar where we had a good view of the place. It was mostly locals, though a few tourists stuck out. Sunlit wasn't known as a resort location. It didn't dock cruise ships like Nassau or Castaway Cay, and the runway wasn't long enough for commercial airliners. Meant the tourists had to come in private boats or small planes. But fishing was likely a draw, and maybe the food too. I sunk my teeth into the first conch fritter our server brought with my beer and immediately ordered another basket. The fritter was just the right amount of crispy and warm, and fresh like you didn't find many places that weren't islands.

"You've still got that bag," Tyson said. "What happened? They didn't let you in?"

"Our soggy friend checked herself out early." I pulled the passport out of the bag and opened to the ID page again. Tyson reached for it and I gave it to him.

"You think she's in trouble?"

I was about to fill him in about my visit to the hospital when we were interrupted by the arrival of a heavyset white guy in a colorful Hawaiian shirt. His belly preceded him by several inches, but his shoulders were broad and muscular. He had an Army airborne tattoo on his left forearm and was thickly built like he could have been a wrestler in his youth.

"You found your missing wingman," the guy said to Tyson and gripped his shoulder like they were old friends. "Who's that you got there? Your damsel girlfriend?"

"This is Coconut Chuck," Tyson said, folding the passport closed again. "He owns this place."

"That's quite the handle," I said.

Coconut Chuck gave my hand an aggressive squeeze, so I squeezed back. "You came in a rare bird, chief. Thing of beauty that Mallard."

"You fly?" I asked.

Chuck released my hand, evidently satisfied with our

impromptu strength test. "Yeah, I buzz around a bit. We keep a Navajo on the field for the business. Put her back together myself from an insurance wreck."

"So the salvage theme is more than show. Real business for you."

"Wrecking is an old tradition around here. Lot of people come out to these islands, no idea what they're doing. Plow off the ends of short runways, run their boats aground. Too hard for most of them to come clean up their own messes. Leaves it to me. A man can do all right for himself if he can use his hands, but it sounds like you know that. Your copilot's been telling us wild tales. Says you netted a couple of unlucky souls out of the drink today on your way in."

"One more unlucky than the other. The pilot didn't make it."

"Sorry to hear that. You know why he went down?"

"Sounds like it might have been a carbon monoxide leak. They're investigating."

"Ah." Chuck rocked back on his heels like he'd seen it coming. "Bad maintenance then. Seen that a time or two for sure. Silent killer. But you said the passenger made it through all right?" He gestured to the passport on the table.

"Seems that way." I slid the passport back into its pocket in the satchel.

"You're not sure?" He cocked an eyebrow at me. Somehow reminded me of the way a hawk might eye a rabbit.

"I'm not a doctor, Chuck. We're just the delivery boys. Cleaning up other people's messes, right?"

Chuck cracked a smile. "Men of action. True enough." He turned to the cute server who had arrived with another round of drinks. "You put these boys' drinks on the house tab tonight, Kate. Never let it be said that Hooper's Haven doesn't know how to treat its heroes."

Tyson's face lit up like he'd won the lottery.

When Chuck walked away, Tyson held up a hand for a high-five. "I told you this was our night!"

I gave him the high-five on principle, but as I sipped my new beer I curbed my enthusiasm. In my experience, a title of 'hero' may earn a few free drinks, but sooner or later, it always comes at a price.

EIGHT
SIDE SLIP

TYSON WAS LISTING HARD to one side across the booth from me, but it hadn't slowed his mouth any.

"That owner, Chuck. He's ace. I love that dude."

I'd set two glasses of water in front of Tyson in the last half hour, but he'd touched neither—though he had spilled some reaching for his free cocktails. I guess the old saying applied to horses as well as teenagers. You could lead them to water, but not forestall their hangovers.

"Yeah. Chuck's a generous guy," I said. "Though maybe he ought to provide free ibuprofen in the morning."

Our ever-faithful bartender/server, Kate, had slowed her service, taking pity on Tyson's young liver, but he was still smitten with her, grinning his cheesing smile every time she got within ten feet of us. I decided it was time to leave while he still had some dignity intact.

"Let's save some drinks for the rest of the island," I suggested.

Tyson wrinkled his lip. "It's early, though. It's only . . ." He checked his wrong wrist for a watch, then found it on his other arm. "midnight."

"And we've got flying to do tomorrow. Later today now, technically."

"I'm just gettin' my rizz going, man. That Kate's starting to feel me."

"I doubt she wants to see those drinks she served you come back up though." I rose from the booth and waited for Tyson in case he needed steadying.

A busser was standing nearby with a bin ready to clear our table and I had a feeling the night was winding down for everyone. A few old-timers still lingered at the bar but the place had mostly cleared out.

Tyson managed to find his feet okay and followed me to the bar at a wobble.

I paid the bill for the food we'd consumed and left a generous tip for Kate to factor in all the drinks we'd enjoyed for free. She gave me an appreciative smile.

She brushed my hand with hers as I was retrieving my credit card and spoke softly. "Hey, that pilot you said died. Was he a young white guy? Kinda blondish hair?"

"Yeah."

"I think he was in here yesterday morning. Bought a sandwich and asked to use the phone. Said his cell plan didn't do international calls."

I put my wallet away. "Not a local then."

"Crazy he's dead. He was so young." She shook off the thought and turned to my inebriated ward. "It was good meeting you, Tyson. You come back soon now."

"Oh, you know I will, baby." Tyson only slurred a couple of the words.

Glass shattered behind us and someone swore. We turned around to find the young busser on the floor with the contents of his bin all over him. He'd evidently slipped in a puddle on the worn hardwood floor. He attempted to get to his feet too quickly and accidentally slipped again, this time sticking his hand in some of the shattered glass.

"Whoa, hey there. Hold on," I said, navigating the broken glass to help him up.

"Damn it," the young man muttered as I lifted him to his feet. "That one got me good." He opened his hand to reveal a chunk of glass imbedded in his palm.

"Oh boy. That's going to need stitches," I said.

Kate called Chuck over and he had a quick look. Kate fetched a clean towel to staunch some of the blood. The young man was dripping red and adding more mess on the floor.

"I'll drive you over to the Solomon Center," Chuck said.

"No!" the young man exclaimed. "I'll call my brother. He'll pick me up."

"Your brother's all the way on the south island. Be twenty minutes at least till he gets up here. I can take you in three minutes, get one of Doc Marcus's people to have a look at you."

"No. I won't go there. I'll wait for my brother. He'll take me to Mama Jacqui." The young man reached into his pocket with his good hand and found his cell phone, then walked out of the mess to the front door clutching a cloth napkin to his wound. He sat gingerly on a chunk of piling out front that made up some of the nautical decor.

"What's with the aversion to the Solomon Center?" I asked Chuck. "That's twice today I've seen someone get upset about going there."

"Superstitious folklore," Chuck said. "Bunch of nonsense."

"The place has a curse," Kate interjected. "Is what they say anyway."

"Who's Mama Jacqui?" I asked.

"Nobody," Chuck said.

Kate looked like she wanted to say something, but she must have thought better of it.

I helped them gather up the debris and offered to pay for the damages. "Pretty sure that was our spill he slipped in."

"Hazard of doing business," Chuck replied, waving away my offer. "He'll be fine. And we have more cups and plates. You get your protégé home safe. I think he's proved his mettle for the night."

I thanked Chuck and guided Tyson out the nearest door and into the street. Looking back, I saw the busser still clutching his hand and staring down the road, waiting for his ride. Kate came out to check on him. She gave us a half-hearted final wave.

The night was cool and dry and stars shone brightly overhead on our short walk. The lack of light pollution put many thousands more stars on display than we had on the mainland. Tyson looked up and marveled at them too, though he may have been seeing even more via double vision.

"Man. This is lit. Can you imagine living out here? All these stars. The drinks, the ladies. When I finish my certs, I ought to come out here and work for Chuck. Bet he could use a good mechanic."

"You definitely made an impression," I said.

Inside the motel room, Tyson managed to get his shoes off before crashing into the nearest bed. He declared into his pillow that he only needed to rest for a minute, but after that his movements were minimal. By the time I'd changed into a T-shirt and some athletic shorts to sleep in, he was already snoring softly with his mouth open.

I filled a couple of water glasses. I left one on the nightstand next to Tyson's bed, then took the second with me out to the small balcony on the back of the room that I could access via a sliding glass door. I took the old satchel with me too and set that on the patio table, having a seat and propping my feet up on the opposite chair before taking in the view.

Our room overlooked the town as opposed to the beach, but it was still an interesting view. Only a few lights remained on in nearby houses, but the entrance to the Solomon Center was visible and glowed brightly. Farther south, the island's terrain was lost to darkness for several miles, but then, far in the distance, a few more lights shone. At least someone in the south island village of Pelican Roost was still awake.

I dragged the weathered satchel onto my lap and opened it. I pulled out the passport first, reexamining the photo of Fabienne Thompson. She stared at the camera with a look that bordered on defiance. Her jaw was set, her full lips pressed together in a line. The image had a sense of strength to it, determination in her eyes. She certainly didn't give off the impression of a person who was a shrinking violet. Yet somehow seeing this island earlier today had made her scream and lose consciousness. The carbon monoxide and near drowning likely had more to do with her passing out than her constitution, but something about the mere sight of this place had stolen her breath. The second she had it back, she'd run.

I felt inside the satchel and pulled out some of the blue file folders it contained. They'd had time to dry since my first viewing, and now they were easier to open. The first file was that of a woman named Esther Marcelin. She was in her sixties according to the date of birth. Her place of birth was listed as Port Au Prince, but the document I was looking at was labeled with the name of a medical facility in Saint-Marc, Haiti. I recognized some numbers that might have been blood pressure and pulse rates, but I couldn't read anything else because none of it was in English. I thumbed through a few of the other files and they likewise showed names of men and women from Haiti. Claude Jean-Baptiste, Marie Pierre. Kednaud Joseph. Not all from Saint-Marc, but all with Haitian city names. There had been a signature on each file but the seawater had smeared them beyond legibility. All of them were medical records, but indecipherable to me.

I also found a few yellow file folders in the satchel, though these had been tinted slightly green from their contact with the blue files. These yellow-green files were from Sunlit Cay. The Solomon Center specifically. These patients didn't match any of the names in the other files. They looked like Americans, from what I could surmise based on names and addresses. These files were in English at least, but if there was a correlation between the two groups, I couldn't see what it was. There was one last file in its own plastic sleeve. It was printed on paper with a different header that simply read, Pelican Roost Medical Clinic. The file was older, dated over fifteen years ago, but I recognized the patient name: Ruth Solomon. The diagnosis being treated was advanced cirrhosis. Liver disease.

There was one other item in that file, a photo of a team standing in front of a Haitian medical clinic. Dr. Marcus was in the photo, as well as Mali Solomon who was putting up a peace sign with her fingers. A few other nurses or doctors filled out the group. I studied the photo for a few seconds, then slid each of the files back into the bag, none-the-wiser for the exercise.

Maybe they were just routine medical records. There had to be digital backups somewhere. How important could they be? But if they were unimportant, why bother to fly them somewhere? And what did the Solomons have to do with it?

I took one last look at the passport. It was fairly new. US.

I pulled out my phone and tried Googling Fabienne Thompson. None of the social media results matched the woman in the photo, but after several pages of digging, I found a listing for a nursing school scholarship winner. The article looked to be a few years old, but the spelling of the name matched and the vaguely out-of-focus image of the smiling recipient looked like it could have been her. The nursing program was on the east coast of Florida.

What was she doing in the Bahamas? Vacation? Job?

I thought about the little red-and-white plane's circling descent to the waves. The distressed radio call.

Something about the situation rubbed me wrong, but I couldn't put it into words.

A yawn escaped me and I checked my watch. Well past a reasonable hour for sleep. I stepped back inside the room and found my way to the bed, leaving the screen door open to let in the balmy night air.

It had been a long day. Certainly eventful enough. I ought to have fallen straight asleep once my head hit the pillow. But it took me a long time to fade out. And once asleep, I only dreamed of planes sinking deep into oceans.

NINE
FINS TO THE LEFT

I WAS up at first light and on the hunt for good coffee.

The Windy Palms motel brochure claimed it offered food somewhere, but it turned out to be an unapologetic display of browning bananas and yogurts of a questionable vintage, so I went walkabout.

The village of Hooper's Haven evidently came alive slowly, but it had charm to spare. The homes were quaint and colorful in the morning sunlight, small wood-sided bungalows with welcoming porches and brightly painted shutters. I found a cheery bakery a short walk from the motel that lured me inside with the smell of fresh donuts and flaky croissants. The woman working the bakery gave me an extra chocolate-filled pastry with my order just for the fun of it, saying I couldn't leave town without trying her personal favorite.

I pulled Fabienne Thompson's passport from my rear pants pocket along with my wallet and showed the picture. "You ever see this woman come in here?"

The baker shook her head. "She's not from Hooper's Haven, or I would know. Could be a tourist. Friend of yours?"

"Recent acquaintance. Just trying to return some lost things that belong to her."

"Can probably leave them with Constable Swain if you need to. He could find her."

"That may be what I do if I can't find her soon. You know of someone named Mama Jacqui?"

"I do. She's been on the island a long time. Delivered both of my babies. They're grown and gone now so that gives you some idea how long she's been working."

"You must be a liar, because you don't look old enough to have two grown children."

That got a smile out of her. "You're supposed to compliment me before I give you the free éclair."

"We're just doing everything backwards. Know where I can find Mama Jacqui?"

"Got a clinic in Pelican Roost. Just off the main road past the stop sign. Hard to miss it. Something ailing you?"

"Not yet. But it's never a bad idea to know a doctor. Especially after I eat all this." I lifted the bag and pretended to struggle with the weight of it.

The baker shook her head and wagged a finger at me. "My pastries are lighter than air and you better tell everybody so."

I thanked her with a smile and departed.

The coffee from the bakery proved worth the walk, and I took it on a tour of the neighboring streets while I sipped. The place reminded me a lot of nearby Hope Town, minus the lighthouse. But I'd had enough of lighthouses lately anyway.

Hooper's Haven did boast a small library, a grocery market, and several golf cart rental places. I wandered up to one where an old man with a bushy white beard had a cart jacked up and was replacing the rear wheels.

"Can you get to the south end of the island by golf cart?"

"Could if I had any left to rent. They've all been booked for the week. Assuming that storm don't scare everyone off."

"How about this one?"

"It's due to be rented too, this afternoon."

"It's a long time till afternoon. I'm sure I could get it back by then. What if you have one of these pastries I just bought, and I'll put those wheels back on for you while you think about it?" I took a bite of one of the still warm croissants and offered the bag.

He must have been able to smell them from where he stood because he wandered over to have a look nose-first. "I guess it wouldn't hurt to have a taste."

I handed them over.

The golf cart was old and the jack was older, but the wheel change wasn't much trouble. I had the cart back on the ground in about five minutes.

The owner of the place had finished off a donut and was eyeing the interior of the pastry bag again.

"I guess I could part with that cart for a half-day rate. Provided you have it back by noon."

"You'll see me sooner than that." I wiped my hands off on a rag, then pulled the chocolate éclair out of the bag. "But take this off my hands so I don't have a coronary."

"If you insist."

I gave him some cash for the cart rental too and he waved as I rode off. He already had chocolate in his beard.

Tyson groaned when I opened the curtains in the motel room and let the daylight in.

"Why you so mean, man? I'm dying over here."

"Good morning, sunshine. We're headed out."

He managed to get upright and smacked his lips a couple of times. "Did I lick a bag of cement last night?"

"You should shower. You smell like a gas station bathroom."

Tyson rubbed his forehead. "That bartender did me dirty. How you let her do that to me?"

"Oh, all those drinks were her idea, huh? Meet me downstairs at the golf cart in ten. We'll find you some food." I gathered up the old satchel to deliver and headed back to the door.

"Here I thought we were friends."

Fifteen minutes later, Tyson trundled down the stairs, still squinting behind his sunglasses, but freshly showered and smelling of Calvin Klein body spray. He had the sense to bring along a bottle of water.

"Where'd you get a golf cart from?"

"Santa Claus."

I switched it to forward and tapped the accelerator as Tyson was still getting seated. He flopped back against the seat with a grunt. His disposition improved some when he found the remaining croissants.

The golf cart was governed to a decent speed so we made okay time, leaving Hooper's Haven behind and heading south on the sandy main thoroughfare.

"What makes you think this chick is even on the south island?" Tyson said.

"She ran out of a perfectly good hospital on the north side. Had to go somewhere. South island is the farthest she can get without getting wet. Plus it turns out she had a file in her bag with the name of a clinic down there. Made me curious to check it out."

"Remind me why we care what she's up to? We already dragged her ass outta the ocean. How many times we gotta be her heroes?"

I considered that, then adjusted my grip on the steering wheel.

"Once when I was a kid, I visited this bay in Central

California. A nature conservancy group was re-releasing a sea lion they'd saved from a prop strike and rehabilitated. I guess it had taken a couple of months. There was a local TV station there for the release, documenting the sea lion heading back into the wild. Everybody felt good about it. They were watching that sea lion swim away, cheering and shouting, and then right as the TV cameras were watching, zooming in for a final shot, an orca came up and chomped it. Bam. No more sea lion."

"Oh shit. Oops."

"Yeah. Oops."

"That's just like, nature though, right?"

"Sure. But those 'rescuers' didn't exactly do that sea lion much of a service by not checking the water for orcas first, did they?"

Tyson nodded. "You think our sea lion could be in orca-infested waters?"

"I don't know. But before I fly away and congratulate myself on being a hero, I'm at least going to check for fins."

TEN

MAMA JACQUI

PELICAN ROOST WAS a town of few frills. Its primary feature was a fish market and a marina. Fishing boats bobbed in the light waves at a public dock, though several were out of the water for repair. The waterside road was in need of fixing too, the pavement eroded by the surf to half a lane wide in places. We found the single stop sign the baker had mentioned, and it wasn't a long search to find the clinic belonging to Mama Jacqui.

The block house had an address and a mailbox and a simple sign out front that said "Medical Services."

Tyson had done some Internet digging on the ride down and discovered that Mama Jacqui was a licensed nurse practitioner and specialized in pediatrics. The few photos available showed a grandmotherly woman with cheerful eyes and a bright smile.

I expected the same when I knocked at the front door of the little clinic, but found the door locked and no one responded to the bell.

Tyson and I stood on the narrow front porch in the morning sun and waited. I was about to give up and leave when the door finally opened a fraction of an inch.

A graying head was barely visible beyond the crack.

"What do you want?"

"Hi. I'm looking for Fabienne Thompson."

"What for?"

"You know her then."

"I didn't say that."

I tugged at the strap of the satchel that I wore over my shoulder. "I have something that belongs to her. Looking to give it back."

"What makes you think she's here?"

"Found her passport in the bag. She was headed somewhere yesterday. Probably still headed someplace, but she ran out of a medical facility on the north island. Just want to see her, make sure she's okay."

"Saved that lady's life," Tyson added.

The door opened a bit farther and she squinted at me. "You're the pilot. Heard about you." The old woman was the same Mama Jacqui from the Internet photos, but she wasn't smiling or looking especially grandmotherly. Looked like she might knife somebody.

"If she's around here somewhere, we'd like to talk to her and give her things back," I said. "We've got to fly out today, and we don't have a lot of time."

"You can leave the things here. I'll see if I can find her."

"Can't do that. Best I can tell, these are private medical records." I patted the satchel. "You know what she's doing with them?"

"If they are private medical records, you shouldn't have them either."

"Fair point. But best I can tell, Fabienne is the one who can sort things out for us. I would've given them to her last night, but she checked herself out of the Solomon Center in a bit of a hurry."

Mama Jacqui didn't have a uniform on. She wore a loose-fitting floral top and black skirt. Her sandals were on but her toes were sandy. The sand was vaguely pink. She appraised me and then addressed Tyson. "Who are you?"

"The copilot."

"They're making them young these days. I can't help you, gentlemen. I'm sorry." She began to close the door.

"Hang on," I said.

She paused.

"If you see Miss Thompson, please tell her we'll be at The Boneyard restaurant up by the airport till lunchtime. Then we're flying out. If I don't hear from her, I'll consider leaving her things with the local constable. Maybe she can pick them up from him."

Mama Jacqui's eyes narrowed again, but she nodded and closed the door. A deadbolt jammed home.

Tyson met my eye. "That didn't give me a bunch of warm fuzzies about our girl."

"Me either."

We walked back to the golf cart and sat.

"What now?"

"No idea."

I hit the accelerator and we drove around the small town of Pelican Roost. We got some curious stares from locals. A few nods. Not many smiles. The disparity in income compared to the north island was evident. Several young men hung around idle on street corners. No one was sleeping on park benches, but the lack of any parks or benches had something to do with that. A local all-age school let out for recess and a few children came outside to play on sun-faded playground equipment. Even the children seemed to regard us with suspicion as we rode past. I waved. Only one little girl waved back.

Maybe I should have showed up in the airplane. That would have won them over.

Overall, the town looked run down and in need of a paint job.

"Well this was fun." Tyson said. "Can we leave now?"

"Not yet."

I circled back around to Mama Jacqui's place and eyed her home and office from a distance. It was an island of its own. A man in his forties with very few teeth and shaking hands hobbled his way up the steps to knock meekly on the door. It opened and he was admitted.

I wasn't a cop, or a doctor, but it seemed to me that Pelican Roost had itself a drug problem. At least some of its citizens did. The medical office of nurse Mama Jacqui was obviously a key element of life here as a result. What goes up, comes down, no matter the high. At least this guy was seeking help.

Did Fabienne Thompson suffer the same malady?

"She'd been out this morning," I mused. "A lot of sand in her sandals. Hadn't been home long enough to clean them off. Where do you think she went?"

"The nurse lady? Anyplace. Doing her job, probably. Out to breakfast? Could be anything."

"She has a truck out back. Think maybe she drove somewhere sandy?"

"We on an island. Sand could be anywhere."

"Not here though. We just did a loop all over this village and I didn't see one place sandy enough to where it would be on top of your toes. And the sand on her toes was pink."

Tyson screwed up his face. "You trying to be like that TV detective guy, getting all into minute details to solve your case and shit?"

"Sherlock?"

"No. Not that old. Who's that one guy you're being like? You know that guy from TV."

"Columbo. Spenser. Rockford. Magnum P.I."

"Those names sound made up. I'm talking about a real detective like on an actual show from modern times."

"And yet you're doing it so poorly. Monk? Harry Bosch?"

"Never mind. I'll think of it. The point is, they get real clues and all you got is sand on her shoes."

"Toes. The sand was on her toes."

"So maybe she was walking barefoot in the sand and put her sandals back on after."

"Like after walking on a wet beach."

"So she went to a beach. Could be a zillion reasons she went to a beach. It's a nice day. She lives in paradise. Why not?"

"Sure. But let's keep an eye out for pink beaches on the way back. Maybe we'll visit one too. See what the fuss is about." I stomped on the accelerator pedal again and launched us back up the road.

Tyson rested a foot on the low dash. "You think she went to see someone? What makes you think it's even the girl we want?"

"I have no idea. But she knows her. That's more than can be said about any of our other leads. It's thin but it's not nothing."

"Better pull out some better detective shit than that," Tyson said. "Otherwise this gonna be an unsatisfying conclusion. Unlike your boy, whatshisface."

"Phillip Marlowe. Sam Spade."

"Huh?"

"Jessica Fletcher. Veronica Mars."

"You ain't even detecting the right gender anymore."

"All you've given me is 'detective from TV.' It's my source of information that's letting me down."

"Maybe it was a movie, actually, now that I think about it. Hey. That looks like a pink beach." He pointed.

And sure enough it was.

ELEVEN
ROAD RASH

THE SAND WAS the pinkest at the water's edge. I'd seen the effect before. There were a couple of beaches in the islands that really played up the 'pink sands' angle in their marketing. Here it was more subtle. The color came from a kind of coral insect. They died and their tiny crushed bodies mixed in with the sand and colored it pink. Probably a depressing place if you were a coral insect. Gorgeous for the rest of us.

The beach here was small, quiet. On the mainland it would have been built up and exploited by now. That was another nice thing about the Bahamas. There were so many breathtaking places to be found that even the greedy opportunists couldn't spoil all of them. At least not yet.

Tyson browsed around the waterside, pointed out a crab.

If anyone had been here yet this morning, the sand didn't show it. No footprints besides ours.

I admired the view for a bit, then wandered back to the golf cart. We might be striking out on clues to the missing Fabienne, but it was a nice way to waste our time.

The noise from the truck came first, then the old pickup

swung into view from the main road. It was white and battered. An early 2000s Chevy. The bed held fishing gear. Lobster traps.

The truck pulled right up behind my rental cart and the doors opened slowly. Two guys got out. They didn't look especially friendly.

"Morning," I offered.

The driver was older than his passenger, maybe forty compared to twenty-five, but I was guessing. The driver wasn't huge or especially intimidating, but I couldn't help noticing that his passenger friend had pulled an aluminum baseball bat from the back of his truck.

"You're not from around here," the driver said.

"Just checking out the sights. Nice beach."

The driver looked me over. He had a weathered quality to him. A lot of hours in the sun. But a rigid posture. Ex-military I'd bet. He pointed to the satchel. "I'm gonna need you to hand that over."

I stood next to the cart and rested a hand on the roof. The satchel was beside me on the seat. "What exactly do you think is in it?" I asked.

"Something that doesn't concern you."

"That's interesting. Who does it concern?"

Young Guy with the baseball bat eased his way around the front of the truck. He had some muscles. I'd give him that.

"Got an early morning tee-ball game today? Hope you two are the coaches. Might be unfair otherwise."

Tyson was still a dozen yards away but wandering back, curious.

"Give that bag to us. Nobody gets hurt," the driver said.

"I've actually been working on delivering that damned thing all morning."

"Good. We'll deliver it for you. You can be on your way."

"What's going on up here?" Tyson asked, finally within earshot.

"These gentlemen want to help us deliver our package."

"They know that Fabienne chick? Great." But after he said it, he spotted the bat. He tensed and moved closer to me.

The mention of the name made a slight change in the older guy's face. Not recognition. New information? Maybe he hadn't known her name yet.

"Bad news, guys," I said. "Unless you've got some evidence that you're the owners of this stuff, I can't give it to you."

"I got some fucking evidence for you," Baseball Bat Guy said and slapped his palm with the bat.

The statement lingered in the air.

It was a little over the top and I think we all knew it.

"Here's what I think," I said. "If you were ready to roll us, you would've done it first thing. I think you talked a good game to somebody, maybe figured we'd be easy to intimidate, but if your threats don't work, then what? It's a small island. If you really beat up a couple of helpless tourists, it will get around fast. How long till Constable Swain comes to find you?"

The name caused a narrowing of the eyes in Driver Guy. He knew that name at least. But I assumed everyone knew the only constable on the island.

He wasn't backing down though. "Your friend here is young." He lifted his chin toward Tyson. "You don't want to see him get hurt, do you? So hand over the bag."

"What's this got to do with me?" Tyson asked.

"Your friend is being stubborn," the driver explained. "You should talk some sense into him."

The guy with the bat stepped closer. "You ever been hit with a bat, kid? Broke a bone?"

Tyson was practically standing in my shadow now. But he reached past me and snatched up the satchel, clutching it to his chest. "Young means fast, bro. I got my sneaks on too. What now?" He did a little stutter step and backed up a few feet.

The two guys shared a glance. Probably didn't expect a footrace with an eighteen-year-old.

Tyson's play got a grin out of me.

The two tough guys didn't look amused.

The guy with the bat made a feint in Tyson's direction, but Tyson put the cart between them. Driver Guy looked pissed. The guy with the bat made another move, going around the opposite side of the cart from me, rushing to get to Tyson, but I ducked under the cart's roof and went straight through it, tackling the guy at the waist before he could make it around the cart. He went down to the sandy asphalt with me on top of him. Tyson bolted for the beach, darting away with the bag. The guy I'd tackled tried to get up, but I hit him with a quick right-cross that caught him in the face and sent him down to the asphalt again. Then I had my hands on the bat. He felt me yanking at it and clutched it to him. Then I got hit by Driver Guy who plowed into me from behind. We all went down in a heap.

Two-on-one was less than ideal, but I'd had a good breakfast and was feeling scrappy.

Driver Guy was older, tougher. He threw a solid punch from his knees that I barely managed to deflect with a forearm before he delivered another shot to my ribs. I absorbed the hit, returned a punch and rolled away, scrambling to my feet, and just in time because Bat Guy was up too and coming at me with the Louisville Slugger. But he swung it like he was chopping wood. I caught the bat on its downward arc and moved with it, rolling my arm overtop and turning my back into the guy. He was bound up now. Tyson was a dozen yards away, frozen in place, watching.

I gripped the bat to my chest and then cut loose with my right elbow, smashing back into the guy's eye socket behind me. He let go of the bat and backpedaled, hands to his face.

I spun around and brandished the bat at the other guy. He'd been too slow to gain his feet. I could have taken his head off right then, but I only made a little check-swing to make him flinch.

He gave me a look of hate but didn't try his luck.

The tide had turned. He was smart enough to know it. I let him get to his feet.

I stayed in my batter's stance, weapon at the ready, but they were done. The one whose face I'd smashed spit onto the pavement and swore before retreating back to the truck with his buddy.

"Yeah, what now?" Tyson taunted from the sand. He'd pulled his phone out and started recording.

The younger guy gave him the finger before climbing back into the truck. I considered hurling the bat at them as they backed out, but it wouldn't have proven anything.

Instead, I just watched them go. The green-and-white license plates on Abacos islands are usually easy to remember since they are only a few digits, but the truck stayed in reverse far enough up the road that I never saw it.

Tyson walked back over to me with eyes wide. "That was crazy, dude. You kicked those guys' asses."

"Hardly." My blood was pumping though, and a part of me that I didn't like admitting to was vaguely sad the fight hadn't lasted longer. Nothing quite like a fistfight to wake you up in the morning.

"That was so cool, the way you smashed that guy right in the face."

"When in doubt, hit 'em with your elbow."

"I was about to get in there too if you needed me." Tyson balled his fist. "But it happened kinda fast, you know?"

"You did the right thing. Stay far away from those guys. They'd have hurt you."

"I don't want you to think I'm a chickenshit."

"Easiest way to win a fight is to stay out of a fight," I said. "But I'm sure you'll have my back if we need it."

"Damned straight." He nodded vigorously. "Next one." He put both fists up again. "But hey . . . real talk. Do you think we gonna have a next one?"

I rubbed some sand out of a bloody scuff on my elbow from the asphalt. "Hard to say. But I know one thing. This island just got a lot less friendly."

TWELVE

SHINE

WE ARRIVED BACK at the motel parking lot by midmorning and I was about done with this place. Despite the altercation at the beach going more or less our way, I knew we should go. If it had been just me, I might have enjoyed a bit more of the tension. But I had Tyson's safety as my responsibility too.

I pointed up the motel stairs and directed Tyson. "Head up there and pack our stuff for us. I'm going to get a head start on filing a flight plan. We'll wrap up our business and get to the airport."

"You're not letting those dudes scare you off, are you? You straight up took their lunch money."

"Doesn't matter. We're not here to scrap with locals over some beef we aren't involved in. Your grandparents trust me to keep you safe. Getting into fights isn't part of our agenda."

"We took care of ourselves. Well, you did. You're like that old dude, Rocky Balboa. I'm gonna get you to teach me. I'll be your Adonis Creed."

"Let's teach you how to hustle first. Go run some stairs."

Tyson popped out of the cart and threw a couple punches in

the air. "Pop pop. Let's go!" He jogged to the stairs and launched himself up them two at a time. He tripped at the top and had to put a hand down to catch himself. "I'm good! Gonna work on that."

I shook my head and pulled out my phone, navigating my way to the Foreflight app to start my flight plan home. I was only partway into entering the flight details when Tyson shouted from upstairs again.

"Yo, Luke! I think you should come see this."

He was standing in the open doorway of the motel room holding something in his hand. I climbed out of the cart and hiked up to join him. He met me in the hallway and handed me the piece of paper. "Somebody jammed this in our door."

The slip of motel stationery had the neatly printed words "Whitney Gilton from the Miami Herald called for you." written on it.

It listed a phone number beneath the message.

"You figure that's about us saving that girl?" Tyson asked.

I looked the piece of stationery over again and reread the note. Not much to go on. But based on our last twenty-four hours, the guess made sense.

"Maybe we'll get our names on the news," he added.

As I was standing there contemplating calling the phone number, an SUV pulled into the lot. It bore the insignia of the Royal Bahamas Police Force. It parked in a space next to our rental cart and Constable Swain got out.

"We've got company," I said.

Tyson hooked his thumbs on his waistband in a cowboy stance. "We thinking sea lion or orca?"

"I guess we'll find out. Go get us packed up."

I stuffed the note into my pocket and descended the stairs. Tyson lingered only a moment on the balcony, then vanished indoors.

Constable Swain met me at the base of the stairs.

"Mr. Angel. I'm glad I caught you. You disappeared on me last night."

"Any luck finding your runaway patient?" I asked.

"Not yet. But there's something I'd like to talk to you about. I had a call back this morning from the Air Accident Investigation Authority. They requested to speak with you. They're hoping you can provide a more precise location for their recovery efforts."

"They're going after the plane?"

"If it's recoverable. May depend on the depth. Mr. Baum has generously volunteered his salvage services. You might've met him. Goes by 'Coconut Chuck' over at the bar."

"We owe him for a few drinks last night. Handy you have a salvage operator on the island."

"Mr. Baum runs occasional dive charters for the tourists as well so he knows these waters better than anyone. Diving and salvage overlap often out here."

"He mentioned the islands can be hazardous to out-of-towners."

"Only the reefs, we hope." His eyes roamed to the golf cart. Fabienne's satchel still sat on the seat, along with the baseball bat I'd recently acquired. I walked over and plucked the bat from where it was leaning, then handed it to the constable.

"Speaking of hazards, I ran into a couple guys this morning who misplaced this. Drove a white pickup truck with a bunch of lobster traps in the back. They seemed to be having trouble maintaining your island's hospitality standards."

Constable Swain took the bat. "Lobster traps? I might know the truck. They gave you a hard time?"

"Nothing serious. But I can't say I appreciated the attention. Those guys have a reputation for causing trouble?"

"If it's the gentlemen I'm thinking of, they do all kinds of odd jobs around the island. Sometimes work as security for Mali Solomon. What was the issue they had with you?"

"They tried to rob us, but it didn't go well for them."

"That's serious. I'll have a word with them. Are you looking to press charges?"

As he was speaking, my attention was pulled skyward by the unmistakable sound of two turbine engines. The shiny Embraer Phenom 300 passed overhead and streaked out to the west in a wide turn.

"Ah," Constable Swain said. "It seems Ms. Solomon has returned."

The plane's landing gear extended and it came around for the final approach to the runway. The chrome inlets on the turbine cowlings flashed in the sun.

"She flies nice hardware," I said.

"I'm sorry you ran into trouble here." Swain returned his attention to me. "I promise I'll look into the issue. But can I convince you to stay to help us with the recovery of the missing plane? Your knowledge of the accident will be especially essential. We'd like to attempt recovery quickly before the storm and currents have a chance to move the wreck."

"I've got other responsibilities to tend to back home as well."

"That's understandable. But you can see how essential your account will be to the investigation."

"You said you called in the Air Accident Investigation Authority. Are you sure it was an accident?" I asked.

Constable Swain cocked his head at the question. "You know something I don't?"

"Not necessarily. But the doctor said the pilot died from carbon monoxide poisoning. That seem odd to you?"

"The blood tests were conclusive."

"But it was a Cessna 182. The most likely cause of carbon

monoxide poisoning in a small plane is an exhaust leak into the cabin heat shroud."

"Sounds common enough."

"In summer? With a new exhaust system? They wouldn't have needed the heat."

"What makes you think the exhaust was new?"

"I saw the plane go belly-up. Spotted the exhaust through the damaged cowling when I was diving for the pilot. It was as shiny as one of Solomon's toys."

"You saw this under water?"

"Oddly enough, it was about the shiniest thing down there. And exhaust stacks don't stay that way long. They'll patina from use within a hundred hours."

The constable looked toward the airfield and the sound of Mali Solomon's private jet. The aircraft landed and deployed its thrust reversers. Had to be a good pilot if they regularly managed to get in and out of the short strip.

"I'm not an aviation expert," Swain said, "but there must be other ways for carbon monoxide to leak into the cabin. Besides the scenario you described."

"Maybe. I'm sure your investigators will figure it out. Just had me thinking."

Swain nodded. "I'll keep it in mind."

Tyson emerged from the motel with our overnight bags slung over each shoulder and jogged down the steps to join us.

"Have you had any more contact with the woman you pulled from the plane since last night?" Constable Swain asked. "Miss Thompson?"

"None."

"I think that's for the best. I'd suggest you be careful around this particular young woman. We have some questions about what she was doing on the island in the first place. She may have been involved in some suspicious activity."

"Like what?" Tyson asked as he tuned into the conversation.

"I had a report of a woman matching her description that may have impersonated a nurse at the Solomon Center in the past few days. And she might have absconded with medical supplies or other items. It's possible she was stealing pharmaceuticals."

"If we see anything, I'll certainly let you know."

"You still have her passport?"

"I do."

"What do you intend to do with it?"

"If I don't hear from her before we take off, I'll drop it in the mail. Send it to the US embassy in Nassau."

He nodded. "I'd like to see it one more time first if you don't mind. Note the number and details in case she comes looking for it."

I reached into the satchel and fished out the passport for him. I held it while he snapped a photo of the ID page on his phone. Constable Swain retreated to his vehicle after. "I'll let you two consider your plans. But please be in touch before you leave the island."

I gave him a two-fingered wave as he climbed into his car.

Tyson dumped our bags onto the golf cart next to Fabienne's satchel and watched the cop leave. "You didn't want to offload this thing to him to get rid of it?"

"Might do that," I said. "But I'm still figuring out how I feel about that guy. Plus I've got a call to make first."

"He made it sound like he wants us to stick around. We staying?"

"I don't know yet."

I waited till Constable Swain's SUV was out of sight before pulling the note from my pocket.

"You ever heard of this Whitney Gilton person?" I asked.

By the time I had the phone number typed into my phone,

Tyson had googled her on his. He held up an article from the Herald with her photo.

"Chick looks legit."

The attractive blonde staring back at me from the photo rocked slim glasses and a no-nonsense focus. She looked familiar. Her byline was on an exposé of a crooked South Florida politician. I'd read it. It was a brutal takedown.

I dialed the number for Whitney Gilton, but it went straight to voicemail. I was waiting for the prompt to finish so I could leave a message when a text came through.

>>> Can't talk right now. On a plane. Who is this?

I texted back. <<< Luke Angel.

>>> The pilot. Good. I'm on my way to Sunlit. I'd like to hire you for a flight out tomorrow. Back to Miami.

I texted back. <<< I'm planning to depart today.

The little typing dots appeared on the screen as I waited for her reply.

>>> $10K good enough to keep you there overnight? Send me your details. I can do half in advance.

I studied my phone. Huh. Ten-thousand dollars would buy a lot of avgas. Especially since I was headed that direction anyway. Could help fix a few things on the Mallard too. I looked up at the sky, blew the air out of my cheeks, then looked back to Tyson.

"What is it?"

"Put our bags back in the room. Looks like we're here another night."

Tyson's eyebrows rose. "Another night like we can hit up that E. Z. Breeze party now?"

"I forgot all about that."

He gave me his cheesiest grin. Waiting. Eyes like a damned puppy.

"Fine. We'll go."

"YES!" He pumped his fist. "Now we *livin'* that island life."

I wasn't looking forward to socializing with the selfie crowd, but I could suffer through it.

I texted the reporter back. >>> Okay. For 10K I'll stay one more day.

She immediately sent a link to enter bank details.

Tyson danced his way back up the stairs with our bags.

Overhead, the clouds shifted and obscured the sun.

One more day. How bad could it be?

THIRTEEN
BONEYARD MARINA

THE RESTAURANT of The Boneyard Bar and Grill had a healthy lunchtime crowd. The back deck tiki bar overlooked the marina, but the tables with a waterfront view were all full. Tyson and I managed seats at the bar instead, and Tyson viewed the drink menu with a hint of caution this time.

Coconut Chuck himself was behind the bar today. "Hair of the dog?" he offered.

"I'm still kind of fuzzy from last night," Tyson replied.

"Gotta grab that bull by the horns. Right back in the saddle."

"You have anything that doesn't come with animal-related metaphors?"

"Here. Take a shot of this. Good for what ails you." Chuck poured a short glass of amber liquid and set it in front of Tyson, then turned to me. "How 'bout you, Cap?"

"Iced tea."

"You're in paradise. You want to spend time in paradise drinking tea?"

"Thought the British built their empire in these islands on the merits of tea," I countered.

"I think you mispronounced it," Tyson interjected, tasting his drink and smacking his lips. "It's pronounced sla-ver-y."

I nodded. "Fair point."

Chuck filled a glass of ice with tea from a pitcher and set it in front of me. "Here you go. Tea with a side of white guilt. Enjoy. Want a lemon with that?"

"Technically, he only gets that half-white guilt," Tyson said. "His momma was a sizzling hottie from Mexico. I've seen pictures."

"That a fact?" Chuck said. "Been to Mexico a few times. But it didn't agree with my digestion. What's your other half made of?"

"Regular Florida assholes, mostly," I said. "A side of the family tree best not mentioned."

"Few of those on my tree too," Chuck said. "Though mine are from Chicago." He leaned on the bar. "What's Mister Half-An-Asshole want for lunch?"

"Grouper sandwich. Blackened." I handed back the menu.

Tyson ordered the fish tacos and Chuck left us to put in the order.

A seagull landed on the barstool next to Tyson and canted its beady eye at him, studying his drink.

"This ain't for you. Shoo!" Tyson waved a hand and the bird flapped off the stool a few yards and glared at us from the deck.

When Chuck came back he was holding a marine chart and laid it on the bar in front of me. "The good constable was by this morning. Says you're the man I need to talk to if I want to find that Cessna that went kerplunk."

"Salvage operators work quick around here."

"If I don't, the insurance company'll get the outfit from Nassau to do it. I'd like to keep this one local."

"Your bartender from last night said she saw the downed pilot in here yesterday. You meet him?"

"May have, now that you mention it. Young guy. Low-time pilot out of South Florida. Seen him in here a few times."

"His own plane?"

"No. A rental. A company from the states has a loose one over there. One of those dial-and-rent situations. No official school. Just an app."

"We have one of those based at Whitted, too. Thought I saw a US registration on this one as it went down. That's common?"

"Almost always. There's a school in Nassau, but the planes are all US registered. They hire mechanics with FAA A and P certificates to work on them. Why duplicate all that work with the US and the FAA so close?"

"Makes sense." I fished my phone from my pocket and located the screenshot I'd taken of the crash location. It didn't take me long to pinpoint the spot on Chuck's nautical chart. "Here."

Chuck craned his neck to read the depths and I turned the chart back to him to make it easier.

"Damn. Picked a spot right at the edge of the shelf to sink it, huh?"

"It wasn't the shallows, unfortunately. How deep can you dive?"

Chuck scratched his stubbled chin. "Depends. If it's right on this spot, could still be shallow enough. You see it hit bottom?"

I shook my head. "Saw the shelf, though. Plane looked like it was doing a header into a mountainside at night."

"Could be it's still there then. Might be sitting at fifty meters. Or it banked away from the mountain as it sank and now it's a mile down."

"Irretrievable at that depth."

"Unless the insurance company wants to get real spendy and spring for a bigger sub."

"You've got a submersible?"

"Two-person Triton good to three hundred meters. You can see it out there." He pointed to the largest vessel in the marina. A round yellow submersible sat in a rig on the stern.

"Nice setup."

"Sixty-two feet of salt and barnacles, but she gets the job done."

No barnacles were visible from where I sat. In fact, the craft looked pristine. There was even a teenager out there scrubbing it. My knowledge of boats didn't extend much to salvage vessels, but a boat that size didn't come cheap. The salvage business must have been lucrative. That or Chuck sold one hell of a lot of fish sandwiches.

The seagull made another attempt to land on the stool next to Tyson, and he was forced to shoo it away again.

"Pesky bastard, isn't it?" Chuck said.

"Never knew an alcoholic seagull," Tyson said.

"You two are welcome to come along for the ride out to the wreck today," Chuck said. "You ever salvage a plane before?"

I nodded. "We've fished a few out of Tampa Bay. One of the runways at Whitted is short and people like to splash the occasional 172 off the end."

"Student pilots?"

"Sometimes. Though you'd be surprised. Once in a while even high-time pilots forget the basics. Had one coming all the way up from the Keys that ran her own plane out of gas and landed it a hundred feet short of the sea wall. Guys with control locks left in, oil caps left off. I've seen all kinds of blunders when you fish the planes out. Mostly non-fatal thankfully. Bruised egos usually the worst of it. Turns into a project dredging them out of the water though. Luckily Tampa Bay is only a dozen feet deep most places. Nothing like you're diving for. Curious to see *that* plane though."

"Why's that?" He folded his chart.

"Should be able to figure out exactly what happened. A pilot makes a mistake on land, sometimes they try to cover their tracks. One time I had a guy that crashed a plane into the side of my maintenance hangar. He came taxiing back at high power and clipped a wing right into the edge of the hangar door. Luckily no one was hurt. Claimed his brakes failed. Only I'd seen him out there taxiing at high power the whole time. Idiot had left the parking brake on and got the brakes so red-hot taxiing around that he melted the o-rings in the brake calipers and all the hydraulic fluid leaked out. We ran over to help, and I caught him fighting to stow the parking brake handle back in. He'd figured it out just as he was shutting the engine down. If I hadn't seen him trying to cover it up, his story of blaming the failure on the maintenance shop might have worked." I held up a finger. "But, the ones who go into the water never have enough time to cover up anything. Too busy swimming. You pull the plane out of the drink, you'll see the issue right where they left it. Control lock still in, fuel selector set to 'off,' whatever it is, it's still there."

Chuck crossed his arms. "You think this dead pilot did something stupid too?"

I sipped my iced tea. "This one's strange. Pilot died of carbon monoxide poisoning in the summertime. What would they be doing with the cabin heat on?"

"I see your point. Exhaust shroud heater. But you said it yourself. Pilots make all kinds of mistakes, especially in an unfamiliar rental plane. Reach for the cabin air, mistake it for the cabin heat. Accidentally don't push it back in all the way. There you go. There's your CO inlet."

"Could be. But you'd still need an exhaust leak into the shroud in the first place. Otherwise they'd have just been hot and not poisoned."

"Exhaust could have been leaking for three months and this guy was just the unlucky son of a bitch to turn the heat on."

"Yeah. Maybe. I'm just curious what you'll see when you drag it out of the water."

Chuck was staring off at the horizon with his brow furrowed. Seemed to be mulling something over. When he turned back to us he brightened again. "Bet your food's up. I'll go check."

Tyson slid his empty drink glass back across the bar. "I think Chuck was right. I do feel better. Whatever that was, it was delicious."

"Better pace yourself, or you won't make your party."

"Hair of the dog, Chuck says."

"What about 'drunk as a skunk?' There's an animal metaphor for you."

He shook his head. "That one doesn't make sense either. Who ever saw a drunk skunk?"

Chuck returned with the food and the smell of blackened grouper sandwich erased all thoughts of mystery or metaphors from my mind.

"Turns out I won't be able to host you on the boat today after all," Chuck said. "Forgot I promised a couple local guys the job and we'll be working quick to beat the weather."

"No problem," Tyson said with his mouth half-full of taco. "I get seasick anyway."

I shrugged. "Next time."

The seagull got a burst of enthusiasm at the sight of the food and made another run at the stool next to Tyson. But as soon as it landed, it thought better of it. Chuck had pulled something from under the bar that looked like an ornamental blowgun. The seagull took one look at it and flapped its way back off the barstool. But not fast enough.

Chuck had the blowgun to his mouth and puffed a lungful of air through it.

The seagull took a hit from the dart and went down flapping on the deck.

"Oh shit," Tyson blurted out. "You just kill it?"

Chuck lowered the blowgun and eyed his handiwork. "Nah, it's not dead. Tourists pitch a fit if I kill the bastards." He brandished the wooden weapon. "Picked this baby up in Guatemala. Use them all the time down there." He lifted a glass jar with tiny darts in it. The tips were all soaking in some kind of hazy fluid. "Took me a while to get the formula right for seagulls, but it won't bother you for an hour or two now."

"Holy shit, man," Tyson muttered. "That's legit."

Chuck grinned. "Enjoy your lunch, boys." He scooped up the folded nautical chart, tapped the blowgun once on the bar, then strode off for the dock. A minute later he was aboard his boat.

The seagull lifted a groggy head and blinked as Chuck disappeared from view.

"That guy's wild," Tyson said and took another bite. "But this taco is bussin'."

"Sometimes it's like you're speaking another language. But if that means good, I agree." My grouper sandwich wasn't going to survive long either. Whatever delicious sauce it had on it was getting all over my fingers, and I was looking forward to licking it off.

I eyed the drowsy seagull with a vague sense of guilt. I considered saving it a piece of fish for its troubles. But the bird needed to find itself another island.

Overhead, a plane engine purred softly and a Piper Malibu dropped gracefully out of the sky toward the runway. We were close enough to hear the chirp of the tires on touchdown.

I followed the plane's progress as it taxied off to the ramp.

Looked like Sunlit Cay had a new arrival.

FOURTEEN
HOOPER'S HAVEN

WE'D RETURNED our golf cart before lunch so Tyson and I worked off our meals with a stroll around town. The place was hardly a shopping Mecca, but Tyson found a clothing store that met his standards and he came out of the dressing room wearing an outfit that somehow looked like it was shouting. The colorful shirt buttoned all the way to his neck was only half tucked at the waist. The narrow pants were too long by two inches but bunched at the shoes. He swung a jacket over one shoulder. "Now we're ready for a party."

"You remind me of the '90s," I said.

"I'll take the compliment. '90s are back, baby."

"Never said I liked the '90s."

"What did you get?"

I displayed a sports coat I'd found to dress up the clothes I already had on.

"Oh, regular fashion icon over there. Don't you know? Clothes maketh the man."

I got out my wallet at the register. "Some men, maybe. But you left off the rest of the quote. 'Naked people have little or no influence on society.' Mark Twain. It's satire in case you haven't heard of him."

"That can't be the right quote."

The pleasantly plump woman at the register piped up with a smile. "It's actually Shakespeare, too."

"How's that?" I asked.

"'Apparel oft proclaims the man.' Hamlet. I taught English to high schoolers in my younger years."

"Ah. There you go," I said. "She knows better than me."

"Old Billy Shakespeare, huh?" Tyson puffed his chest.

"You saw what he wore, though," I added.

Tyson shot me a glare.

"I'm messing with you. You look good. That style suits you."

He grinned. "Thought so."

The cashier gave me a smile. "I always liked the Twain quote as well."

"Might not be true, though. Naked people have influenced me plenty."

She blushed. "Me too."

Tyson and I strolled back into the daylight and headed for the motel to drop our belongings. I slung my jacket over the satchel I'd still been toting around.

"I think that girl was digging you flirting with her."

"Not flirting. Just getting a smile out of her. Doesn't cost anything to make people laugh."

"How come you always know how to talk to girls about books and stuff?" Tyson asked. "They all seem super into it."

"I read a lot. Murphy likes it."

"You read to your dog?"

"He's actually partial to memoirs, but dogs have questionable taste in literature."

"You're messing with me again."

"I do have a lot of time to read on the boat at night."

"Thought you had something cooking again with your ex-old-lady. She ain't been around?"

"Cassidy is back in Boston. Not sure where we stand at the moment. I've never been good at long distance."

"She's an airline captain, though. And you're a pilot. What's long distance to you two?"

"Boston is always long distance from Florida."

"She's fine as hell. You should go up."

"Maybe. But . . ." I paused to get the thought straight in my head. "Sometimes loving someone means understanding your capacity to cause them pain. Makes you act . . . cautiously. We've had enough hurt in our relationship, and I'm not interested in causing her more."

"'Cause you don't want to leave Florida."

"That's a lot of it. But if it's meant to work out eventually, it will."

"That sounds lazy to me."

"I'll take that under advisement."

We'd made it up the stairs at the motel, but as we approached the door, something was off. The door was ajar. No sign of a room service cart.

Tyson reached the door first. "What the . . ."

The room had been tossed. The beds were askew, drawers pulled out. Both of our bags had been dumped out. Clothes littered the floor. Someone had worked the room fast and sloppy.

Tyson picked up his flight logbook from the floor. "Damn, man. What the hell." It had the heel of a footprint on one of the open pages. "Sonsofbitches got all up in our shit."

"Check your stuff and see if they took anything. I'll talk to the front desk."

When I reached the lobby, the same guy from the night before was on duty. He was cleaning the coffee machine. He had a name tag on this morning that read "Kaleb."

"You have camera footage on that upstairs hallway?"

The young man looked up, then frowned. "What for?"

After my explanation, he bit his lip. "So, bad news is, the cameras are on a timer. They only switch on at six p.m."

"Not helpful. Why?"

Kaleb shrugged. "It's not a modern system. Needs upgrading, but the owners haven't gone for it yet."

"You see anyone up there this afternoon? Talk to anyone about us?"

"Nobody came in. You had that call earlier. I left a note in your door."

"Yeah. I got it. What about the parking lot? You have a monitor that watches that?"

"Nobody out of the ordinary."

"How about a white pickup truck with lobster traps in it?"

"Yeah, I've seen that truck. It was this morning though. Maybe nine? Before I got that call for you."

"You know those guys?"

"Sure. Vaughn and Jacob. They sell seafood they catch to the restaurant. Figured they had a delivery."

"Constable Swain said they work security for Mali Solomon."

"Probably do. She's not always here, but she's back now. Hosting some kind of party tonight."

"Any of her other guests staying here?"

He thought about it too long.

"That's a yes."

He frowned. "I can't give out names. Motel policy."

"Who has keycards to the rooms?"

"Only the usual. Front desk, housekeeping, and the night watchman. We code all the customer keys day to day."

"You have an explanation for how someone got into our room?"

"Are you sure you locked it?"

I glared at him. He shrugged. "I'll find out. You calling the constable?"

"I'll leave that to you. Do better, Kaleb."

"Not like it's my motel, man. I just work here."

I walked out. No new information. I looked down at the satchel I still had at my hip. Thing was starting to irritate me. Nothing else in our room made sense to bother about. We'd barely left anything in there. What the hell was so damned important about this thing?

When I got back upstairs, Tyson had put the room mostly in order. I emptied the satchel out on the bed and arranged the files by color, the ones from Sunlit on one side and the ones from Haiti on the other. Tyson picked up one of the yellow files and tried to decipher it. "Is this supposed to be French?"

"It's Haitian Creole."

"You understand it?"

"Not remotely. I only recognized the city names."

Tyson attempted to use the Google Translate app on his phone but Haitian Creole wasn't an option. After a thorough perusal of the blue files, I still had no information. Other than the majority of procedures had been surgeries done in the past few years.

Tyson put his hands on his hips. "Are you sure this is what they were after?"

"What else would they be after? Unless they think we have something we don't."

I picked up the satchel itself and gave it another examination. It had several compartments, including the small zippered one I'd found the passport in. As I examined that, I noticed it still maintained its shape, even empty. Probing the pocket with my fingertips, I felt around the edges, then turned the bag upside down till the flap of a pocket flipped over. On the back side, high up by the seam, the fabric had been separated. The inner liner of the pocket and outer canvas of the flap made a second pocket of sorts and when I felt around inside, my fingertips struck something firm. I'd assumed it was some sort of hard plastic backing, but I pulled it loose and discovered it was a second passport.

This one was darker blue and read REPUBLIQUE D' HAITI PASSEPORT above the coat of arms. When I opened it, the photo on the identification page was still Fabienne Thompson, but younger by a few years. And the last name listed wasn't Thompson, it was Jean-Baptiste. The name gave me pause. Where had I read that before?

I went back through the files on the bed, first the blue, then the yellow. It was the third yellow file I checked. The name read "Claude Jean-Baptiste. The words at the top of the form read "Sètifika Lanmò."

Tyson's Google search brought up a translation. "Death Certificate." He showed me the screen.

"So maybe this whole thing is something personal for our Miss Thompson," I said.

"Okay, now we starting to be more like that movie detective for real. Making family connections and stuff. Hold up. I think his name was French sounding too."

"Inspector Gamache."

"Nah. It's that famous white dude actor." He snapped his fingers. "Sounds like an old plane name. The plane from St. Pete."

I gave him a frown. "Benoit? Benoit Blanc?"

"Yeah! That's him. You're like Florida Benoit Blanc."

"The whole parade of film detectives I listed and you can't remember Daniel Craig?"

"You know how white dudes all look the same." He gave me a cheesing grin.

I shook my head. "If I'm going to be a character in one of his films, I'd rather be Bond. Cooler cars, more girls." I sighed and went back to staring at the files.

Claude Jean-Baptiste.

Fabienne Jean-Baptiste.

Death certificates in Haiti. Surgeries here.

There was something afoot. But what was worth all the hassle of tossing our room for it? Who could this benefit? Or maybe the question wasn't about benefit. Who did it threaten?

I stuffed the files back in the satchel. "Come on. We're going."

"Going where?"

"We're going to find Fabienne Thompson. Or whatever her name is."

"We already looked. And we don't have a golf cart anymore."

"We don't need a golf cart. We've got a plane."

FIFTEEN
FLYOVER

THE MALLARD'S engines came to life. Deep, guttural pops and a loping cadence became a steady throbbing hum. Round engines had something in their rhythm that sang of wide open skies and adventure—flying for the pure joy of it. It was a song my soul knew well.

Tyson donned his headset in the copilot seat next to me. "You know this is crazy, right? This ain't a police chopper."

"Ever since we've been here, people keep saying 'It's a small island.' If it's so small, we'll be able to cover all of it quickly."

"Unless she indoors."

"Yeah. But I've got a trick for that."

I taxied *Tropic Angel* to the end of Runway 9, made my radio call, and pulled onto the centerline. My hand on the throttles pressed forward smoothly and the twin Wasp engines responded. Temps all looked good. The RPMs climbed and we were rolling. The Mallard was a loud plane on the ground, but it was pure sex in the air. It had been invented for splashing around islands like these. As we lifted clear of the runway, Hooper's Haven dropped away and we hit our first bump of turbulence. Wind shift. I raised the gear, reset the flaps, and trimmed the elevator. At three hundred feet, I banked right.

Coconut Chuck's tiki bar occupied the prime beachfront real estate on this end of the island with the marina beside it. His salvage yard took up several acres around it to the south. Those fell away behind our right wing and we hit a stretch of public beach with a handful of tourists on it.

I leveled off at five hundred feet.

The Solomon Center loomed large on the bluff beyond the beach with the rest of Hooper's Haven's colorful houses sprawled nearby. That public beach ran maybe two hundred yards before sheer rocks made the waterfront impassable. Another beach sat beyond the bluffs, this one empty and lonely. It stretched maybe half the distance of the first before yielding once more to forest and rock. A handful of block homes sat upon the bluff. If there was a road out to them, it was a narrow one, obscured by trees.

"All right. As good a place to start as any," I said, and dipped the nose, aiming directly above the cluster of homes. I aimed for two hundred feet, idling for the nosedive, then gunning the throttles again just as I overflew the rooftops. The roar from the engines was sudden and deafening.

"You trying to piss off all the locals at once?" Tyson asked.

"Classic barnstormer trick. Nothing like the sound of a plane buzzing your house to get you outdoors to look around. It's how I got all the pretty girls' attention in high school."

Tyson held on as I brought the Mallard around in a steep turn for another pass.

"You and I had a very different high school experience."

"Binoculars time," I said.

He pulled the binoculars from next to his seat and trained them on the homes as we came by again. "Okay, we got a couple faces. Damn. You were right. Four out of five houses came out to look."

Even without the field glasses, I could make out the people who'd wandered outside. Hands lifted to brows to shield the sun for a better look at the dive bombing seaplane. Tyson pulled his phone out and started recording from his dash mount phone holder. "They don't even look that mad," he commented from the copilot seat. He continued his scan with the binoculars too. "But all those people twice as old as our girl. No Fabienne."

I spared an extra hundred feet of altitude this pass and rocked the wings in a wave to the onlookers as I soared overhead. Then we continued south.

The coastline curved, bending east to a point and we overflew the luxurious estate of Mali Solomon next.

"Don't tell me you're going to dive bomb this girl's house," Tyson said. "I don't need my face on the news."

"Something tells me Fabienne isn't tight with Miss E. Z. Breeze."

"Oh damn. She got her own pickleball court. Two pools. Is that a nine . . . ten . . . twelve car garage?"

I spotted a security guard at the gate and two more roaming the grounds. Two catering trucks were parked in the drive, and an event planner. Staff with armloads of table cloths and bottled booze gazed up at us as we cruised over. Party prep was in full swing.

"What's that over there?" I pointed to the southeast side of the estate where the coastline drifted toward the west again. A small cottage sat among the trees beyond one of the golf course fairways. A woman was outside on a deck overlooking the driveway. A shiny white SUV sat in the drive. Might have been a Lexus. Exhaust floated from the rear of it. A man was inside but his features were obscure.

"It's somebody." Tyson aimed the binoculars at the woman. "Not Fabienne though."

The woman watched us pass. She had a frail quality to her and a crimson scarf in her hair that waved in the breeze.

"Oh shoot. I think I know who that is," Tyson declared. "That's Ruth Solomon."

The home was neatly ordered with a pretty garden along one side, but small overall. Mali's mother evidently lived in a more frugal style than her daughter. Not that it was hard to do. I circled the cottage once while Ruth watched, then leveled out again. Whoever was in the Lexus didn't make an appearance.

As we cruised down the shoreline, we passed another house, tucked back into the bluff above a thin crescent of beach. The white house paint was peeling and the windows were boarded with plywood.

"People getting a jump on the storm prep out here," Tyson commented.

The landscaping on the property was overgrown, vines climbing up the house. It might have been boarded up for a storm, but something about the place made me think it wasn't a recent one. No vehicles or signs of occupancy. That little stretch of beach was pink though.

Farther south we hit the outskirts of Pelican Roost, the island's smaller settlement. Here we did spot a few people in the act of putting up storm shutters. A few bumps from the wind jarred the aircraft and we were reminded why. I gained more altitude flying over the village, but made several circles. Tyson kept his binoculars trained on the houses. Kids in the schoolyard all watched us with interest.

"There's your girl Mama Jacqui," he said.

The nurse practitioner had come out of her office and watched us with hands on her hips. I waggled the wings. By the next lap she had gone back inside.

"I'm seeing a lot of people," Tyson said from behind the binoculars. "But still no Fabienne."

"She's on this island somewhere."

I overflew the pink beach Tyson and I had stopped at in the morning, dipping so low we were nearly skimming the surface of the water. The tide had washed away most of our tracks, but the reminder of our visit gave me another target to search for. I climbed again and circled the center of the island. It didn't take long to spot the white pick-up truck with the lobster traps in the back. It was parked outside a roadside bar on the outskirts of Pelican Roost. The place had none of the outrageous decor Coconut Chuck's bar flaunted. This looked like a locals-only watering hole. Drinks for drinking sake. No need for an Instagram-worthy background.

I eased the throttles back, dipped, and buzzed that place too. I gave the engines full throttle directly above the bar.

As we came around in a teardrop turn, the maneuver had produced the desired effect. A dozen patrons wandered out to see the cause of the commotion. Some had spilled drinks on their shirts.

Our friends from the pickup truck were among them. I recognized the young muscled dude I'd tangled with and his mentor. The young guy shot us with a finger as we flew over the second time.

"Well, we've got everyone on the island's attention," Tyson said, looking back at the surly crowd in our wake. "Now what?"

I dipped left and adjusted my heading for a course back to the airfield. "We've stirred the pot," I said. "Let's see what bubbles up."

SIXTEEN
THE PASSENGER

HOOPER'S HAVEN AIRFIELD was no longer sleepy when we got back. I'd extended my downwind approach due to two other planes in the traffic pattern. When we landed, there were more on the ramp, a Mooney Ovation, a Cirrus SR-22, and a Bonanza, all high-dollar models with nice paint jobs. The Malibu we'd seen land earlier was taxiing out to the runway for departure.

The weather may have been scaring off a few tourists, but Mali Solomon's party was at least increasing the population of the island for the day.

One of the new arrivals was in the FBO that served as a terminal, and she looked familiar.

The blonde hair and stylish glasses matched her photo on the Internet, and her posture at the counter was a giveaway too. Looked like a reporter if ever I saw one. Taller than I expected, though.

Basil caught my eye and waved me over. "These boys might be able to help you out."

Whitney Gilton turned to have a look at us and let out a resigned sigh. She covered it too late with a forced smile.

"Trouble?" I asked.

"Don't sound so excited," she said.

"Our fault," Basil interjected. "We've only got but a few rental vehicles on this island and unfortunately the last one available is giving Miss Gilton a bit of trouble. One of you boys okay driving a manual transmission?"

I opened my mouth to speak, but the reporter cut me off. "Of course he does. Look at him." She hiked her purse up her shoulder. "And I *have* driven a stick shift, just not recently."

"I can tell we're going to have fun," I said.

"This isn't a rescue mission, soldier. Just a logistics problem. Please don't label me as your damsel in distress."

"Wouldn't dream of it." I addressed the room at large. "Damsels, fend for yourselves!"

She planted one hand on her hip and held out the car keys with the other. "I know I only hired you for the flight tomorrow, but I'm willing to compensate you for some driving services too, if you're agreeable. I assume you got your deposit?"

"No idea. But I trust you." I took the keys.

"You don't even know me. You should verify your bank account."

"Trustworthy until proven otherwise."

"Ah. Another male luxury. Must be nice."

I moved to pick up her suitcase and she got to it first. "It's fine. I can handle it. Thank you, Basil," she said, and laid some tip money on the counter.

"No need," Basil said, and tried to offer it back. "Just doing my job."

"It's yours." She straightened up and fixed me with a stare. "Shall we?"

"After you." I gestured to the door.

Tyson held the door open for her and she let that pass

without comment. But Tyson and I shared a look as we walked behind. Tyson's eyebrows were raised.

With a manual transmission on the agenda, I was expecting we might be squeezing into a Dodge Challenger or some manner of Subaru, but our ride turned out to be a shiny Ford Bronco.

I got the back open for Miss Gilton's carry-on bag and she acquiesced to my tossing it in for her. I'd previously stashed the satchel we'd recovered from the 182 in the bow of the Mallard so for the moment I was unencumbered. Felt nice.

Tyson made a move for the shotgun position, but I warned him off with a head shake and he let our passenger take it. I admired her well-toned calves as she climbed in the front seat.

"Where to, madam?" I asked as I got behind the wheel across from her.

"Trying to find the name of my hotel," she said, scrolling on her phone.

The Bronco was a seven-speed transmission so I skipped first and got us rolling in second gear, assuming first was some kind of rock-crawling mode. Turned out to be the right decision. It was a far fancier ride than my Jeep that I cruised around in back home, but it rode nicely.

"I need to change. Then I'm due to attend an event in an hour at the home of Mali Solomon. I don't think I can get you in, unfortunately. It's a private affair. But hopefully they'll let you drop me off."

"That's okay. We're already on the list." I pulled out onto the road and made a left.

Whitney Gilton looked legitimately surprised. "*You* are invited?"

"Us and E.Z. Breeze go way back," Tyson interjected. "To yesterday. She knows the life of the party when she sees it."

Whitney pivoted in her seat, phone in hand, and studied

Tyson. "Are you two a package deal? I technically only need one driver."

"I'm the copilot."

"Vital part of any crew," I added.

Our passenger did a bad job of disguising her skepticism. "It's just that the job I'm here for is going to involve a lot of discretion, and . . . silence."

"Hear that, bossman?" Tyson said. "She talking about you. Doesn't want you simpin' all over her while she tryin' to work."

"Even if I knew how to 'simp' on her, or what that meant, I'm sure I wouldn't," I replied.

"That's not what I was implying," she argued. "I'm just saying I'm here to meet someone. Alone. And I'm ensuring that we all give each other some space at this event. I'm aware that we will be arriving together, but that doesn't mean we need to *attend* together."

"Copy that," I said. "We'll keep our distance."

I pulled off the road and into a parking lot.

She seemed placated, and went back to her phone. "Thank you. Now if I can just find my hotel name . . ."

I parked the Bronco in a space and shut off the engine.

"Okay, it's called 'The Windy Palms . . . motel?'" She looked up from her phone screen and out the windshield.

I pointed to the sign swinging on the post next to the truck. "Pretty sure it's the only motel on the island."

Gilton stared at me and narrowed her eyes. "You're staying here too, aren't you?"

I shrugged. "Makes life easier."

"Does it?"

We climbed out and I retrieved her bag from the back before she could object. The gusting wind was blowing her hair around, but she brushed it away from her face. "I've got your number. I'll call you when I'm ready."

"Or find us in the bar," I said, and pointed to Coconut Chuck's place next door.

"Fine. Please stay sober enough to drive."

"That's me. Sober as a stone."

She gripped the handle of her rolling carry-on and marched off to the lobby, still battling the wind.

Tyson eased up next to me with his hands in his back pockets. "That girl's spicy."

"Is that what you'd call it?"

"Fine as hell, though."

"You've said that about every woman we've met this trip."

"'Cause I'm a gentleman. Giving due respect to all the ladies. I'm an equal-opportunity complimenter. Don't worry. If you ever get yourself looking good, I'll tell you."

"You're too kind."

"Maybe when I come visit you in your retirement home," he added. "The bar is lower for old people."

SEVENTEEN
SOLOMON

THIRTY MINUTES later we were showered and dressed and sitting at the bar at The Boneyard watching the wind take the tops off the waves in the channel. The Bahamian flags flying on the backs of sailboats in the marina were flapping straight out. I eyed the clouds hustling by overhead and wondered how rough our flight out would be in the morning. Right now the winds were straight down the runway, but it was already blowing harder than forecasted.

Coconut Chuck's salvage boat was still gone. Made me wonder how the recovery of the Cessna 182 was going. Tyson was sipping the dregs of some cocktail that had come with a teal swirly straw and was endeavoring to keep the straw out of his eye while getting the last of the ice chips.

My lime and soda sat mostly untouched, but I'd helped myself to half the basket of conch fritters before Miss Whitney Gilton appeared in the doorway. Her hair was up now, with braids that wrapped around to prop up a messy bun in the back. Smart hairdo in the wind. It was the lavender dress that was the eye-catcher. Her lacy collar went up her neck and featured a sort of choker tie. With long vaguely sheer sleeves and a flowing bottom, precious little skin showed anywhere, but the lightweight material and tailored lines of the outfit cut a stunning figure nonetheless. Maybe it was the glasses, but somehow she managed to look breezy and serious simultaneously. Like a vacationing librarian.

"Are we ready?" she asked as she found us.

"Unless you need a drink first," I offered.

"Probably," she said. "But I'd rather get going."

"All work and no play trip."

"My editor is expecting greatness."

I got off the bar stool and left cash for our tab. "This story of yours is about Mali Solomon's charity work?"

"Yes. That's right." She slid her phone into her clutch, then snapped it shut again.

"More PR about her magnanimity to the islands? What's the hook?"

"I guess you'll have to wait and read the article, won't you."

"Huh. Interesting."

She eyed me carefully. "What?"

"You're doing a negative take. Didn't expect that."

"I didn't say it was going to be negative."

"Didn't have to. It was all over your face. I suggested it was a puff piece and you didn't try to defend it at all. Means it's not the regular Solomon fan fluff."

"You're making wild assumptions, with zero evidence."

"He does that," Tyson said. "You should see what happens if you got pink sand on your toes."

Gilton studied him. "If that's a joke, I'm not getting it."

"Had to be there, I guess."

She sighed. "Okay, well if we're done being obscure and unhelpful, are we ready to go?"

I pulled the Bronco key from my pocket. "Your carriage awaits, my lady."

"Please don't call me 'my lady.' This isn't a date."

"Your carriage awaits, dude."

She let out a sigh and walked out the door.

We departed Hooper's Haven and wended our way south on the short drive to Mali Solomon's estate. The side road wasn't marked, but it was the only offshoot of the main road in the vicinity of our target, and my guess was proven correct when we rolled up to the broad gates of Solomon's driveway.

There wasn't a full-time guard house, but someone had been posted at the gate today for the event. The gate stood open but the middle-aged security guard leaned in the window to survey us briefly before confirming our names and identification. On an island this remote, I didn't imagine there were a lot of dangerous party crashers to fend off, but I couldn't begrudge the guy his job. He checked Tyson and my driver's licenses without fuss, but paused on Whitney's ID and studied her. "With the Miami Herald? This is a non-press event."

"I'm the exception," Whitney said.

He dialed a number on his phone and had a brief conversation with someone.

I glanced over at my passenger. "Had to cause trouble."

"Don't look at me like that. I'm on the list."

The guard finished his conversation and must have heard what he needed to. He handed back Whitney's ID and waved us on with instructions to park around the back of the garage.

"You lied about your story topic?" I asked.

"I didn't lie. But I may have inferred something they misinterpreted." She had a hard time keeping the smirk from the corners of her mouth.

Tyson leaned forward to peer out the windshield as we

approached the mansion. His phone was out and recording. "Looks even bigger from the ground."

I hadn't been to any celebrity homes before, but this seemed to fit the basic bill. It was immense for one person, with tall windows that fanned out to both sides in a modern day tropical palace. The roundabout held a few Ubers that were dispensing glamorous passengers into the waiting arms of staff.

Since our vehicle was staying, we parked behind the garage as instructed and walked around to the front on foot. Whitney strode ahead, repeatedly checking her phone. Club music emanated from speakers in the hedges and only gained in volume when we made it into the foyer.

I was offered a glass of champagne within the first ten feet of the front door, but passed on it. Tyson took two. Whitney turned to me and fixed me with a no-nonsense stare. "Thank you gentlemen for the ride. I'll come find you when it's time to leave."

"Oh, you're wanting space already? I don't think this date is going very well."

"It's not—" she started, but caught herself. "I'll find you later."

Tyson sipped his champagne as she walked away. "You do irritate the prettiest girls though."

"You have to do something well in life."

We turned to assess our options and I did a double-take. "Hang on a minute. Is this whole floor an aquarium?"

"Oh man, this chick is so legit." Tyson got out his phone to take a video of the floor. Schools of colorful tropical fish darted and flashed beneath the glass floor as we walked overhead. "Coolest thing I've ever seen," he declared.

"How do they even get inside to clean that?" I wondered. "Scuba tanks?"

"Yo, I gotta get myself a pic with Mali Solomon."

I watched the colorful fish chasing each other underfoot. "I'm going to find myself a drink that doesn't bubble. I think I'm going to need it."

We parted ways, me making better progress, as Tyson stopped to shoot videos with his phone about every three feet.

The house was large enough that with the quantity of people present everyone still had plenty of room. Guests were gathered in clumps in strategic locations. A catered bar anchored the scene in the spacious living room/aquarium area. The bartender wore a vest and cheese cutter hat that lent a vintage vibe to the scene. Four young twenty-somethings were posted on a couch playing a video game on a TV the size of a billboard. The characters in the game blasted away at each other with unrealistically large weapons while base jumping from skyscrapers. A few onlookers commentated from the adjoining couch.

An interior balcony overhung the living space, and when I looked up, I spotted our host, Mali Solomon, in lively conversation with a bevy of admirers. She surveyed the scene below and our eyes met briefly. I got the slightest of nods before she went back to her conversation.

I walked through to the rear sliding doors that stood open. Wind tormented the flames of gas tiki torches scattered around the pool area. I spotted the gaunt frame of a man I recognized in a group gathered by the barbecue. Dr. Julian Marcus. He wore all black. His expression at parties was even more serious than his work face. Maybe he didn't like club music. Our eyes met briefly but if he recognized me, it didn't show.

There was an island in the pool and the music blasting from the back deck speakers had inspired some girls in bikini tops to dance out there. Maybe it was their job. They were good at it in any case, but they looked cold. I wandered around the pool to the secondary bar. The crowd here was older, mostly guys in their forties and fifties looking unsure of why they were here. I could relate.

I ordered a bourbon neat from the bartender and tipped cash. I felt a hand on my shoulder and turned to find a genial older man with a colorful bowtie staring at me.

"Luke Angel. Thought that was you. Burt Ransom."

The name was vaguely familiar.

"You fixed my Meridian in St. Pete once. Fuel flow problem. You had it figured out so fast, I don't think my coffee had time to get cold."

"Burt. Right. How's she running for you now?"

"Ah. Don't know. Sold it. Moved to a Piper Matrix. Insurance was killing me with the pressurization. We only fly over here to our house near Treasure Cay anyway. Got roped into this by my wife. She's involved in all the local charities."

Burt went on to describe his place in the Abacos and the state of the fishing in the islands, but my attention wandered, because coming up the steps from the back garden, a young caterer carrying a tray of empty glasses and plates stopped at the edge of the pool deck to look around. Her vest and black pants were a close match to those of the other caterers, sleeves rolled up to achieve the same casual vintage look, but something in her posture lacked the acquired ennui of most veterans of the service industry. She was alert and bright. On the hunt for more than dirty dishware. Her black hair was styled in a way that it obscured most of her face, but what I could see of it matched a pair of passport photos I'd spent a lot of time looking at lately.

Fabienne Thompson had joined the party.

EIGHTEEN
SIGHTED

MALI SOLOMON OWNED A GONG. Maybe it was synthesized and came over the speaker system, but the music stopped, and the gong noises certainly got everyone's attention. Even Burt was obligated to stop telling me excruciating details about his new beach house. The group I was standing with at the bar all pivoted like a herd of sheep to face the rear of the mansion. Mali Solomon walked out to the balcony overlooking the pool deck and stood several moments with a gravitas fit for a pope. Then she lifted her hands. "What's good, my people? How's everyone enjoying the party?"

She got some generous applause and a few whoops from the pool island bikini girls.

When I looked back to the stairs, Fabienne had disappeared.

I swore inwardly and eased out of the crowd of dudes huddled around the pool bar.

She couldn't have gone far.

I took my bourbon on a slow walk around the pool, keeping to the edges so as not to distract from Mali's welcome speech.

"Everyone here tonight has been a generous donor to our

islands." The microphone in her hand was picking up too much interference from the wind so she ditched it and just yelled. "You all should be proud of yourselves tonight. I know I am! Weather's not going to let me talk too long but we've got a killer night set up for you. My girl, DJ Crash down there is going to keep it going for you, and the drinks will be flowing. Food's all the best of the islands. Get yourself some of that lobster down there. I want to give a special shout out to my man Doc Marcus from the Solomon Center. None of this would ever be possible without you." She pointed to him and waved. He bowed slightly. "We've got Mayor Rolle hanging out, a bunch of others I see have been doing great work. Treat yourselves right tonight, friends. Seriously. From the heart, you all made this happen." She threw up both hands again. "Peace, peace."

The DJ flashed the lights around the pool and the bikini girls cheered again. Then the music started back up and conversations resumed.

Dr. Marcus smiled wanly as a few people patted his back. The woman Solomon had identified as the mayor looked more appreciative of the attention. She shook hands vigorously with the guests around her, all smiles. But Marcus's eyes wandered upward to a window in the adjacent wing.

As the lights pulsed, I noticed the silhouette of a figure in one of the upstairs windows there. It looked like she had been watching the scene from the darkness of an unlit room. But she was standing close enough to the window to make out the red scarf we'd spotted her in from the air. I recognized her as Ruth Solomon. She and Marcus were staring at each other. But as I watched, she faded backward into the darkness and out of sight. Made me wonder what she thought of her daughter's theatrics.

When I lowered my gaze back to the level of the party, I found I was being observed too.

Across the pool, standing at one end off the buffet table, was the driver from the white pickup I'd tangled with earlier. Maybe he was the one who had provided the lobster for this setup. He was wearing a security polo this time, however, and staring knives at me. As I continued around the edge of the pool, he moved too. With my eyes on him, I didn't see his buddy till he was already at my side. The younger, muscled guy looked none-to-pleased to see me either, and for a moment I wondered if he was going to shiv me. He was still wearing sunglasses, despite the sun having set, and upon closer inspection, I realized why.

"Nice shiner," I said. "If it makes you feel any better, my elbow is a tad sore too."

He gave me a scowl. "Better watch it, flyboy. People tend to trip and fall a lot around pools. Might hurt yourself."

His companion was almost to us also, but got held up when another guest stepped into his path and asked him something,

The young security guard reached up and laid a hand on the back of my neck. A bold move since I was taller than him, but he did a little flexing to compensate. "We're gonna go someplace and talk." He pointed with his other hand toward a side gate leading around back of the pool house. There was another security guy waiting by the gate.

Maybe this was going to be a polite conversation, but somehow I doubted it. And if the Army had taught me anything, it was that you never let your enemy choose the battlefield when you can help it. I tossed the remainder of my bourbon back and shifted the glass to my left hand. Then, quick as thought, I reached up with my right hand, grabbed the wrist the security guard had on my neck and ducked under his arm. The maneuver immediately put him in front of me, and with leverage on his shoulder. It took only a quick push to his back to send him stumbling forward, and headfirst into the pool.

The splash caught the guests around me by surprise, but I set my empty bourbon glass down on a neighboring patio table and immediately began clapping. A few of the concerned looks shifted to smiles. One of the pool island bikini girls cheered.

That guy was right about the pool deck being slippery.

By the time the security guard came up sputtering and fuming, I was already moving away in the opposite direction from his scowling companions.

With all the cheering and attention, Muscles Guy was forced to smile and pretend the dive was his idea.

I ran into Tyson as I hurried my way into the house. He was with the gamers on the couch, trying to give advice to a cute girl with a gaming headset on. I grabbed his arm. "Hey. I just spotted Fabienne. She's dressed like one of the catering staff."

"Oh shit, she's here?"

"Help me find her. Fast."

Tyson turned to the girl on the couch. "Be right back, baby." If the girl noticed, she didn't show it. She was too busy driving a tank over some zombies on the giant television.

I led Tyson across the aquarium floor and tried to imagine where Fabienne went. "Check upstairs. I'll head for the kitchen."

"What do I do if I find her?"

"Stick with her, and call me."

Tyson moved off toward the stairs. I checked my six for the security guys, then crossed behind the inside bar and down the hallway in the direction I'd seen the catering staff coming from. There was a hallway to the left that looked like it contained a recording studio. A couple people were in line for a neighboring bathroom.

I tried farther down, and as I rounded the corner of the dining area, I spotted her. Fabienne had just come out of a door that might have led to an office or library. Our eyes met and she froze.

"Hey!" Someone shouted from behind me. I turned to find

the mean-looking security guy from the lobster truck entering the hallway behind me. He pointed. "Stay right there."

Fabienne came unfrozen and ran for the door to the kitchen.

Shit.

I went after her.

The security guy shouted again. "Someone stop him!" He put a hand to his gun, but I was already chasing Fabienne into the kitchen.

A big server from the waitstaff must have heard the commotion or sensed something was off because the second Fabienne sprinted past him, he rounded on me and threw up his hands to block my path. "Whoa now." Guy had to be six five and three hundred and fifty pounds of a lot of flab. Made a sizable road block. But I was no Tinker Bell.

"Coming through, Hoss." I grabbed one of his thumbs and twisted it down and in, bending the guy forward and off balance. It was enough to move him a foot to the left and slam him into the countertop on that side.

"Ow, dude. You're mean," the big guy whined.

"This is called politely aggressive," I said, and sidestepped his considerable mass to keep going. "You don't want to see me mean."

Fabienne had shoved her way through a door at the far side of the kitchen and disappeared.

I dashed out the door three seconds after her and looked around. I'd exited the house and was on the long side of the southern wing. To my right was the back of the garage and I could spot our rental Bronco from here. But no Fabienne.

Damn it. I moved toward the back of the house, checking behind various topiaries shaped into animals, then I turned off the walking path into a low-walled vegetable garden. The kitchen door banged open behind me and I ducked.

The security guard I'd ditched was now standing where I'd

been and faced with the same dilemma. He had his gun unholstered. He looked both directions, but chose to head for the parked cars. That bought me some time. I stayed low and crossed the garden full of raised beds and exited the other side. There was a path on this edge as well and it led down a slight hill past a stable and toward the woods behind the house.

I was tempted to keep searching, but I decided to rely on my ears instead. Fabienne had to be close. I tuned out the din from the party in the back yard and focused on closer sounds. Smaller sounds.

I didn't wait long. Gravel crunched around the side of the stable. Someone moving slowly. I kept the weight on the edges of my feet and made one leap to the clean cement sidewalk that circumscribed this side of the stable. Whoever was around the corner was keeping quiet again. I edged that direction, slow and silent. At the corner, I waited, half-shrouded in darkness.

The sound of breathing came from around the corner. Then clicking. The quiet tick tick tick of virtual keys on a phone. A low volume setting but not silenced. The tapping stopped.

"Damn it. Where are you?" a female voice whispered.

I stepped around the corner.

"Hi there. Looking for me?"

NINETEEN
RENDEZVOUS

THE FACT that Whitney Gilton didn't scream was a point in her favor. But she did jump enough that she had to readjust her glasses.

"Damn it, you scared me. What the hell are you doing out here?"

"I could ask you the same thing, but I figure we're on the same hunt. Let me guess. Is your source named Fabienne Thompson?"

Whitney didn't bother to deny it. "We were supposed to find each other in the house. In an office. But the place has like four offices. I couldn't find her. So I came out here to our backup location." She checked the time on her phone.

"You set up a contingency plan. Smart."

"We had some extra places to try in case things got difficult. But she isn't going to show with you here. And my phone reception on this island has been utter garbage." She looked up and narrowed her eyes. "Wait. Why are you looking for her? Or are you just following me to be bothersome?"

"I've got something that belongs to her."

A flashlight beam swept in our direction and Whitney and I both ducked. Two security guards were making their way along the path at the back side of the stable. One I didn't recognize, but the other was the soggy young guy I'd pushed into the pool. Both carried tasers with their flashlights. Maybe they weren't old enough to carry guns here. I was okay with that.

"Come on," I whispered, and we scurried back into the garden.

The security guards moved our way along the side of the stable and Whitney and I were forced to conceal ourselves behind one of the raised vegetable beds. I dropped to a crouch.

"You think you could find a smaller hiding space?" Whitney muttered, as she was forced to back tightly against me to stay out of sight of the guards.

We stayed low, and I tried to ignore how good her hair smelled. I was aware of the warmth of her back pressed against my chest, not to mention her rear end against my groin. She twisted slightly, out of our impromptu spooning position, but it only made it more like she was sitting in my lap.

A flashlight beam passed overhead, then swept right.

Whitney's face was only inches from mine. She turned and studied me as we waited. "Bet you're loving this."

"You could use some gum."

She smacked me in the shoulder.

"Shh," I whispered.

The security guard I didn't recognize had turned to listen.

Whitney and I stayed frozen, glued together in silence, pulses elevated. Mine wasn't entirely from the threat.

The older security guard I'd tangled with earlier arrived back from the parking lot and met his two companions. He was clearly in charge, his subordinates rallying to his position. They huddled briefly on the path near the side of the house. He gave orders, then they divided forces again, moving off and continuing to search the grounds.

Whitney extricated herself from my lap and straightened her skirt and hair. "Fun as this was, I've still got a job to do. And you're not making my life any easier."

"What does your Mali Solomon story have to do with Fabienne Thompson?"

"That's confidential."

"Does it have something to do with the medical records she was transporting back to the US?"

Whitney startled. "How do you know about those?"

"I found them when I was fishing her out of the water. Been trying to give them back to her for two days."

"You have them? Where?"

"Stashed in my plane at the moment."

"You've got the records." Whitney put her fingertips to her lips. "That changes things. Does Fabienne know?"

"How could she? I can't find her. Girl runs like a deer, apparently."

"She's been busy trying to recreate her work. That's why she's here tonight. Trying to get me more of the evidence I need because she thinks she lost it. She's desperate. But if you already have it . . . then we need to get her out of here."

"What the hell is in this story?"

"Fabienne claims Dr. Marcus is anything but what he seems, and she says she has the proof that Mali Solomon is colluding in all of it."

"Colluding in what?"

"Secrets in need of exposing."

"A couple of her hired thugs did try to get the records off me this morning."

"We need Fabienne. I've got to find her before they do."

"You have any more backup meeting locations planned?"

"Fresh out."

My phone buzzed in my pocket. I extracted it and put it to my ear.

Tyson practically shouted through the speaker. "Yo! I just saw our girl." She ran down the back steps. She's headed for the woods."

"Can you follow her?"

"I'm still upstairs. Saw her out the window."

"Get after her. We'll meet you. Which part of the woods?"

"Toward the beach. East. Uh, maybe zero eight zero."

"Meet us out there."

"Got your location sharing on?"

"I'll add you."

"It's a function on your phone. So I can find you where you end up."

"I'm not ninety, Tyson. I've got it."

"'Just making sure. Your generation gets a little out of touch with the tech—"

I hung up on him and turned to Whitney. "Come on. Tyson spotted Fabienne headed for the woods. We can catch her."

We gave the stable a wide berth, skirting the building to the south, then cutting quickly across a manicured lawn that I soon realized was part of the golf course. I checked the back of the house and eyed the portion of the woods that would have looked like eighty degrees from Tyson's point of view. "This way." I got a location sharing request from Tyson a moment later and accepted it.

"I did not wear the right shoes for this," Whitney muttered as her heels stuck repeatedly in the soft turf of the golf course fairway.

It was dark on the golf course, but not so dark we wouldn't be spotted if we didn't pick up the pace.

"Go barefoot," I suggested after Whitney threatened to turn an ankle for the third time.

"I don't need your advice," she said. But she took her shoes off anyway. She tried her phone again with her free hand but could only swear at it. "How are you getting signal out here?"

"Give me her number. I'll call her."

"I'm not giving you my source's private contact information."

"If she's telling the truth, I'm on your side of this."

"Then you can carry my shoes." She thrust them at me.

Headlights appeared behind her. A gas-powered golf cart with two security guards aboard.

"We gotta go," I said, and grabbed Whitney's arm, hauling her toward the woods. We ran across the remainder of the fairway and through the rough grass at its edge, then into the cover of the trees. But the golf cart was closing fast.

Whitney tried to pick her footing gingerly among the sticks and leaves. "Ow. Damn it."

"We're going to try a new method," I said, and scooped her up and threw her over my shoulder in a fireman's carry.

"What the f—" But her exclamation of surprise was lost when I swung her around and she saw how close the security cart had made it. As I hustled us through the woods with her jostling on my shoulder, she only held on. "You'd better go faster!"

I didn't know if these guys were desperate enough to use bullets to stop us, but I kept as many trees between us as possible just in case.

Flashlight beams soon pierced the darkness around us, accompanied by shouts, so I kept up my speed, diverting at an angle into denser woods. Our pursuers fanned out but they were moving slowly.

My grip on Whitney's knees tightened as I was forced to navigate over a small stream and up an embankment on the far side. We were moving steadily downhill and finally reached an area that was mostly sandy terrain. I set Whitney back on her feet and caught my breath. "You hit those hors d'oeuvres pretty hard on the way through the party, huh?"

Whiney narrowed her eyes at me again. "What, all those muscles of yours are just for show? Sissy on the inside?"

"I'm good now. Who needs breathing."

"You think we lost them?"

I turned and scanned the woods behind us. "No. I'd give us five minutes max till they catch up."

She studied the water in the distance and the little stretch of shoreline we'd hit. "Let's go this way."

I followed.

Her intuition proved sound. The path from here was easier going and before long we'd made it onto a small stretch of sandy beach. Large rocks dotted the sand, but there was enough open space between to walk. And ours weren't the only footprints. Someone had come through ahead of us. The footprints led back into the tree line thirty yards ahead. Whitney was following but something nagged at me. A background sound. A two-stroke boat motor? I listened hard and searched the dark horizon. My eyes strained to see any movement on the water. If it was there, it wasn't using running lights.

The wind and waves were too loud. If the outboard had been out there, it was gone now.

"The footprints go this direction. Hurry up," Whitney insisted.

"Wait. Hold up."

"What? She went this way."

"Something's not right."

"What are you talking—"

But when I turned to the left, her eyes followed mine, to the figure in the shadow of the trees just behind us. To the woman pointing the gun.

TWENTY
PROCEDURE TURN

"WHAT'S HE DOING HERE?"

The gun in Fabienne's hand didn't waver. It was small. I was guessing a .22 caliber target pistol. Not the most fearsome weapon on earth, but still nothing I enjoyed being on the business end of. I put my hands up.

"He's okay," Whitney said. "He's helping me. Some."

The gun stayed pointed at me. Fabienne looked older in this light. Untrusting. Something feral in her eyes. Like the last day on the island had hardened her against everyone. Or maybe she always wore that expression when awake.

"I'm also the guy who pulled you out of the ocean when your plane went down. Maybe you don't remember."

That got more of a reaction. "That was you."

"Same guy."

"Then why were you and that security guard chasing me in the house?"

"Technically, he was chasing me. Still is, I imagine."

She slowly lowered the gun. "There are other people in the woods. I've heard them."

"Then we don't have a lot of time," Whitney said. "But Luke says he found your evidence. The medical records."

"What? How?"

"Dredged up with your pilot," I said. "He didn't make it, unfortunately."

Fabienne's face clouded. "Because she killed him. And she's still out to get me too."

"You think Mali Solomon was behind the plane crash?" I asked.

"She's behind all of it. She and Dr. Marcus."

Whitney took a step closer and took out her phone. She had the voice recorder app open. "I read your emails. I'm ready to listen. So is the Herald. If you really have proof, this is a story the world needs to hear."

"If she finds out what we're doing, she won't let us off this island," Fabienne said. "She's already tried to kill me once."

"To cover up what?" I asked, forced to speak loudly due to the wind and waves.

"The truth. The bloody, dirty truth. What they really do here. Those records? They have the names of Dr. Marcus's victims. The people he's killed. And the people who've profited."

Her delivery was frantic, but she obviously believed every word.

"Most of those records were in Haitian Creole," I said. "How come?"

"Because Haiti's his hunting ground. That charitable foundation they run down there? His medical missions everyone is so proud of? The free cancer screenings and blood tests? It's all a front for his real work. He's illegally harvesting organs from Haitians and selling them here."

"Organs?" I said. "You're saying Dr. Marcus is involved in organ trafficking?"

"Not trafficking. Murder. The names of people I have are just the ones I know for sure are missing or dead. I think he's been killing for decades. Serial murder."

"It's a huge claim," Whitney said. "Your evidence will need to be rock solid."

"It all matches," Fabienne said. "If I can get the story in the press, the authorities will have to investigate. More of the victims' missing family members will speak out. Ones who haven't been silenced yet."

"He runs a huge celebrity-sponsored business," I argued. "If he's got Mali Solomon giving grants to his hospital, why would he need to kill people on the side?"

"Because she's in on it, too."

"Why?"

"To keep up his improbable reputation. Most successful organ transplant surgeon on this continent? It's an industry-wide supply and demand problem everywhere else. But here? Their graft survival rate is ninety-seven percent, three to five percent higher than average, and their waitlist times are consistently twelve to eighteen months shorter than the US. It's because they have supplemental supply sources."

"Can you prove that?" Whitney pressed.

"When I have the records. I can show you. And then we're taking all of them down." Her resolve showed in the firm set of her jaw.

Whitney looked less-than-convinced. I had my reservations too. The idea of Mali Solomon backing a murderous doctor seemed far-fetched. But something was clearly going on to drive Fabienne to this point.

I recalled the name in the files that matched her second passport. Her Haitian passport.

"Who was Claude Jean-Baptiste?"

Her expression changed, softened, and she took a deeper breath. "He was my father."

"You think he's one of Marcus's victims."

Some of the rigidity had gone out of her posture, but her voice was still cold. "My dad lived in a village outside of Saint-Marc. He hated doctors. Refused to see them most of his life. But his appendix burst and they took him to Dr. Marcus's clinic while he was there visiting on one of his 'medical missions.' Marcus operated and saved his life. That's what we all thought anyway. But when he came home to recover, he wasn't the same. He died within days." She looked at Whitney. "I told you all this. In the emails."

"Your father's records say he died of an apparent drug overdose," I said.

"Part of the lie. Marcus and his people killed him. I know it."

"Those files in your bag are from more than just your dad's death," I said. "You found more missing persons you connected to this?"

"I think he flew some of those people here, to Hooper's Haven. That's why they went missing."

I scratched my neck. "If he was out to kill people, why transport some to the Bahamas first? Why not do it all in Haiti?"

"He did kill in Haiti. Plenty of times. But sometimes he'd bring them here first, to prolong the time their organs were viable."

"You have evidence of the flights?"

"No. But I have a video. Marcus's plane. With one of the missing women getting aboard. I took it to the local police in Haiti, but they said there was nothing I could report. She wasn't family. I had no grounds to report her missing."

I knew that to be true. Even in the United States people went missing all the time, and getting anyone to even look for them was a maddeningly slow process.

"We should be able to track that plane with your video."

"But I only had the video saved on my phone and my laptop."

"The phone currently at the bottom of the ocean," I added.

"No cloud backup?" Whitney asked.

"My dad lived in a rural village, not Palm Beach. I was working with what I had. I planned to back all of it up in the states but hadn't had a chance."

Whitney was about to respond when a sudden motion down the beach caught all of our attention. A light. We all ducked behind trees. Fabienne put her gun up.

"They found us," Whitney whispered from beside me.

Fabienne looked like she was about to start shooting.

"Wait," I said. "That's not a flashlight. It's just a phone."

"Luke?" Tyson's voice carried through the trees. "You out here?"

I stepped out from behind the tree. "Over here!" Then I turned to Fabienne. "It's okay. He's with us."

Tyson jogged over and pulled up a few feet away, catching his breath. "Dude. You need to get back up to the house. Some crazy shit is going down."

"Crazy like how?"

"Screaming, yelling. People running, calling for the cops."

"You see why?"

"No, dude. You said to find that chick Fabienne and you. She right there by the way." He pointed to Fabienne.

"Yeah. Great work."

"Hey, girl. I'm Tyson," he said, straightening up and giving her a little head nod. "Remember, from that time we saved your life?"

Fabienne looked to me for an explanation.

"He's always like this. You get used to him."

"We can't take Fabienne back to that house," Whitney said. "It's too dangerous."

"How'd you get here?" I asked Fabienne.

"Dropped off up the beach by a friend," Fabienne said. "But I don't know if she can get back to me now. The water's getting rough."

The waves had indeed increased in tempo and size. If someone had dropped her off by small boat, they'd find getting into the beach a struggle now. Perhaps that explained what I'd heard over the waves.

"There was a road down this way that cuts across the property and exits out to the south. You and Tyson can cut across the woods here to the road. I'll meet you with the truck."

"I'll stay with her," Whitney said.

"I'm going to need you to navigate whatever mess we're getting into up the hill. Run interference."

"Interference." She adjusted her glasses. "Do I look like a linebacker?"

"You've got the thighs to make a cornerback jealous. You'll be all right."

Whitney raised her eyebrows.

"That's a compliment," Tyson explained. "Cornerbacks are hella fast." He turned to me. "When you be scopin' on her thighs though?"

"I had to carry her for the—we should go," I insisted, before Tyson got me into more trouble. I pointed to the gun in Fabienne's hand. "Be careful with that. Doesn't exactly make you look harmless."

"I'm not harmless. And I don't intend to be."

Fair.

"What happens if you don't come get us?" Tyson asked.

"Rendezvous back at the motel."

"Copy that."

He and Fabienne started making their way south, Fabienne keeping him in front of her.

"You think he can keep her safe?" Whitney asked, watching them go.

"She might be the one keeping him safe," I replied. "You believe that story of hers?"

"I don't know. If she has the evidence she says. I'll have to confirm it, but it's certainly not the first time a celebrity faked interest in a charity. I knew Mali Solomon's work in Haiti was mostly a PR stunt. Very few celebrities want to personally get their hands dirty helping out down there."

"But serial murder and organ trafficking? That's insane. And if Dr. Marcus has been doing this for decades like she claims, Mali Solomon would have been a kid when he started. How could she be behind it?"

"She's not a kid now. If she's involved, she needs to be exposed."

She had a point. This island might have been small, but it apparently held oversized secrets.

Fabienne's story was salacious, but something about it didn't add up for me yet.

"You don't believe her," Whitney said.

"I know she believes it, but organ transplants are a big undertaking. A lot of people involved, patient matching, narrow windows of opportunity for the surgeries. If it's true, Marcus certainly can't be doing it alone."

"So maybe Solomon's millions didn't all come from tech like we think. She's young, but anyone can have a dark side. And who knows? Maybe more people at this party aren't what they seem."

The thought didn't make me like the situation any better. I was looking forward to putting this whole island in my distant propwash.

"One thing I do know." Whitney studied the terrain ahead of us. "I'm not having you caveman-carry me back up that hill again."

"Next time, how about you pack your sneakers." I stepped over and scooped her up in my arms, cradling her in front of me this time instead.

She took the treatment silently, adjusting her skirt primly over her ankles before taking a grip with both arms slung around my shoulders. "If I feel your hands going anywhere near my ass, you're fired as my pilot."

"Wouldn't dream of it," I lied. But I minded my footing and my hand placement through the woods.

By the time we reached the fairway of the golf course again, I was winded, but took pains not to show it.

I put Whitney down and she walked barefoot beside me the rest of the way to the mansion. She was finally able to slip her heels back on when we reached the private clubhouse, placing one hand on my shoulder to balance her way into them.

The path to the Bronco looked like it might be surprisingly clear. But Tyson hadn't been wrong. Something was off about the situation.

Lights were ablaze in the back of the mansion, but the music had stopped. For a place that had previously been boisterous and noisy, the silence was eerie.

We found our way to the back pool deck steps, ascending the same way I'd seen Fabienne arrive earlier in the evening. The pool area was vacant. The DJ booth still flashed its neon lights but in time with an inaudible beat.

There was life inside the house, however, people standing in an almost reverent circle, staring at the floor.

Whitney and I shared a glance.

"What the hell happened up here?" she asked.

Curiosity got the better of us. Walking up to the back sliding doors, I felt like we were about to interrupt a seance. A few eyes turned toward us as we entered and I spotted a teary-eyed Mali

Solomon being comforted by another young woman at the far side of the room.

The center of the living area was vacant, and even the fish were keeping to the edges of the aquarium. A few feet into the room, it became evident why. Bobbing just beneath the thick glass of the aquarium floor, floated the lifeless body of Dr. Julian Marcus.

TWENTY-ONE
DEPARTURE REQUEST

THE MOOD WAS SOMBER in Mali Solomon's home. Constable Edwin Swain stood alone in the living area, staring at the couch while the rest of us lingered in the foyer. Swain's phone was to his ear and he listened intently to whomever was on the other side. His uniformed figure cut a stark contrast to the previously glamorous night.

I didn't envy Swain's job. Tiny island or not, the role of lone constable of a remote place relied heavily on the fact that crime on small islands was rare. A woman in plainclothes that I didn't know had helped take statements. She was apparently the go-to deputy for days when Swain was off the island or needed a break, a known fact for the other local guests. But I got the impression this island mostly policed itself.

Whitney Gilton typed rapidly on her phone next to me, fingers flying over the device's keyboard. She'd shot a bunch of videos too. Taken some photos. She'd have been a terrible journalist if she hadn't. Based solely on the location of the death, this story could be international news when it broke. No doubt a slew of other journalists would arrive on scene, sniffing for fresh soundbites. But for now it was hers. Add in the angle from Fabienne's accusations, and Whitney was sitting on an immense story. Despite all that, she didn't look especially happy about it. She was doing the job, chronicling the event, but not necessarily the story she'd come for.

"I need to get this emailed to my editor and start conducting a few interviews," she said to me. "This is going to get crazy."

Many of the guests had left— frightened, shocked, or horrified. Those who had remained were a different mix. They likely shared the shock, but there was an element of macabre curiosity too.

Death could do that.

Primal instincts insist we pay attention when our fellow humans die. Danger is sensed. Hierarchies shift. When the security of the tribe is threatened, behavior changes. Survival depends on it. A few of the younger guests had made their own recordings. Probably already irreverently posting to social media. But others stood still, watching, waiting to see what the elders did. Another primal instinct passed down from history's survivors. Learn from those who have seen death before.

"I heard an argument," a woman beside me whispered. "Downstairs. I would swear it sounded like Dr. Marcus. Did you hear it?"

I shook my head.

"The constable should know, in any case," she reassured herself, adjusting her grip on her purse and waiting dutifully for her turn to be interviewed.

Conversations around the room remained hushed.

Then I was bumped.

Security guard. Lobster traps. He stood behind me and spoke low. "We need to talk. Outside." His young muscled buddy from the pool was behind him.

A small island polices itself.

There were no fewer than six security guards in the room now. Four were conspicuously clustered near me.

Whitney had moved off, working the fringes of the room. At the moment, she was whispering to a female guest near the hall to the kitchen. I doubted she was in any danger here. Too many people, everyone on alert. But the guys surrounding me had an agenda. I'd evaded them long enough. I should have taken off when I had the chance, but now I was out of runway.

I could make a scene, I supposed, call for help, make it difficult for these guys to get me alone. But I had a macabre curiosity too. I wanted a few answers of my own. So I turned and let the security guards escort me out the front doors. We made our way down the steps and around back of the garage. The Bronco we'd come in was one of only a dozen vehicles still remaining.

I only made it partway across the gravel drive before being shoved.

I stumbled forward a few steps, then turned around. It was the young guy I'd knocked into the pool. Figured as much. I'd embarrassed him twice in front of his boss. He couldn't stand for that. His ego and manhood had been bruised. Had to level the scales. The other dudes were backup. Plus he needed an audience. He was bristling for the fight, muscles flexing. He took off his sunglasses and handed them to one of the other dudes behind him.

But it was the older guy who spoke first, without emotion. "Let's get one thing clear. You're going to get off this island."

"But you guys are so friendly here," I said.

"You're going to butt out of whatever it is you think you're messing around in," he continued evenly. "You're going to get in your plane first chance you get, and we ain't ever going to see you in this town again. You get me?"

"Message received," I said. "I was planning to leave tomorrow anyway."

"First light," he insisted. "I'd better see that ugly-ass plane of yours like a speck in the wind."

"Ah, see, now you called my plane ugly. That's bad manners."

"Bad manners. Yeah we do got some of that around here. Jacob's got real bad manners."

Jacob of the Swimming Pool smacked a clenched fist into his other palm like a TV bully. Kid really should have been on a soap opera. All drama.

That was his cue though. He stepped forward, chest swelling, but still looking unsure how to make the first move. My posture was relaxed. Waiting. He'd throw a punch eventually. I wasn't going to give him the justification of saying I started this. But it's awkward trying to hit a guy just standing there. The move from stillness to action. The tension gets to some people. Makes them second guess themselves. He hesitated.

"Go ahead," I said out loud. "You make the first move."

The permission seemed to work. Like I was asking for it now. He swelled a bit more and reared back for a punch. But as he pivoted into it, I let my left fist fly with a jab that caught him in his already sore nose.

"Fuck," he muttered as he staggered back, a hand going to his face.

"Said I'd let you *make* the first move, not land it."

But now he was mad. Embarrassed a third time. The anger got the better of his fear and he came at me fast. His punches were hard enough as they glanced off my shoulders and forearms. With all those hours in the gym, he had to have something to show for it. But I could tell the only fight he'd ever won was with a gym mirror.

You don't learn to fight in gyms. You learn to fight on sidewalks. You learn behind quickie-marts and gas stations. You learned from the older brother who beat the shit out of you because sometimes your dad hit him too and he didn't know what to do with all the anger. You learned to fight to survive. Then you learned it again in war.

But the things you learn in war make you a weapon. The things you learn in war are hard to unlearn.

That's why when Jacob let his hands droop and exposed his head, when his footwork was sloppy and left me room to close, there was part of me that knew I shouldn't take the opening. But that part of me lost to the training. I parried his sloppy punch, stepped in fast, and connected with an elbow to his temple. One of the hardest points in my body hitting one the most vulnerable in his. It was something from a textbook. The way his body went stiff before he fell. The way he hit the ground with a meaty thud, already unconscious.

It was textbook. But you don't learn to fight from textbooks either.

This was a show with an inevitable outcome. More WWE than UFC. I was supposed to be the one to go down easy, take my punishment. I should have let this kid save face. That was in the playbook.

Lying there on the ground, I realized how young he still was. Not that much older than Tyson. Guy just needed to get a few shots in, tack his fragile ego back up. I'd have taken a few bruises, but we'd have all gone home satisfied that the predicted outcome had played out.

Now I'd fucked that up.

I had three guys staring at me. Older guys. Harder guys. I'd failed to take my punishment like a good boy, so shit was going to go sideways. Lobster Traps was ex-military too. He knew how to keep score. That's why when he stepped forward to jab me in the ribs, it wasn't with a fist. It was with his stun gun.

Fifty-thousand volts of electricity coursed through me in a second, locking up my muscles and making me go rigid just like the kid had. My knees buckled and I fell, landing on my side. They didn't bother to talk. Don't know that I could have heard much anyway, face down as I lay in the gravel. The only thing I had going for me was that I'd fallen in a slightly curled over position. Gave me a small bit of protection from the kicks that came next. I got kicked in the back and the ass and thighs and the top of the head. My arms and ribs. At least one guy bothered to lean all the way down to punch me in the face.

I saw stars. But I didn't black out.

The hits kept coming and I felt every one.

TWENTY-TWO
THE MESSAGE

"VAUGHN!"

The shout sounded far away. Muffled through gravel and the throbbing of blood in my ears.

But it was a voice I vaguely recognized.

"That's enough!"

The onslaught of boots and fists around me subsided.

I hadn't moved. Not much anyway. Curled around my vitals a bit tighter maybe. Whatever survival reflexes my body could manage under duress. My head hurt. I could tell that much. Most of the rest of my body probably did too, but I was prioritizing my pain on a first-come, first-served basis. Some of it was going to have to register later.

I got my eyes back open and took in the low altitude view of gravel driveway I currently had for a horizon. A shiny pair of shoes appeared. Then blue pants with a red stripe down the side.

"Mr. Angel. Can you hear me?"

"Mmm, hmm," I mumbled. "How can I help you?" I was drooling a little. Or maybe that was blood. I lifted my head slowly and spat. Okay, yes. Blood. I explored my mouth with my tongue and found the cut on the inside of my lip. I seemed to still have all of my teeth though. That was something.

I groaned and let the arm that was pulling on mine lift me to a sitting position. I found myself staring up into the face of Constable Edwin Swain. A few onlookers had shown up too. A woman in a cocktail dress. A guy in a suit. Must have wandered upon the scene on the way to their car. I probably had them to thank for the stop to the violence, but I currently lacked a way to thank them. They shuffled past and rushed for their sedan.

"I'd like you to get up if you can," Swain said.

The young security forces guy, Jacob, was still on the ground too, though it looked like he was also stirring. His buddies helped him to his feet. He looked around groggily once he was up and his unfocused eyes found me on the ground. "Did I win?" he mumbled.

Sorry kid. Nobody really wins a fistfight. He'd learn that too one day. Everybody loses. Just some more than others. I was topping that list currently.

Swain helped me to my feet. "I see you've been busy."

"Making new friends," I said. "Here I thought you said the reefs were the only danger to tourists."

"Might need to amend that statement." Swain turned to Vaughn. "You'd better have a good explanation for this."

"Private property. We retain the right to remove anyone we see fit. He didn't listen."

I steadied myself and locked eyes with Vaughn. His cold stare was still emotionless. A persistent warning. Message received.

The vibe between Vaughn and Swain was frosty too. The town sheriff versus the private security rent-a-cop. Swain could have invoked the superiority of his badge in this situation, but he didn't press it.

"Mr. Angel. Let's get you inside if you can manage it," he said. His voice was calm, like he'd helped me up from a pleasant sit in a chair, and not a beating at the hands of local thugs. "We'll get you cleaned up."

"I think I'm going to need a new dinner jacket," I said, noting the dirt and blood I'd acquired on my blazer.

"Fairly certain the dress code goes out the window once a dead body shows up in the house."

"You might be right."

He led me to the same door I'd exited earlier in my pursuit of Fabienne. The security guys dispersed slowly in our wake.

The catering staff was huddled in the corner of the kitchen as we walked through. The big chef I'd shoved aside earlier stared the hardest as I limped my way by.

I pointed to my face. "See? They were way more aggressive than me. Not even politely."

"How's this for polite?" he said and shot me the middle finger.

Not polite at all if you asked me.

Swain grabbed a cloth napkin from a catering tray and thrust it at me. "Don't bleed on the floor in here."

The hallway on the other side of the door was vacant and Swain let go of me, satisfied I could walk unassisted. My leg muscles had all recovered well enough from the taser shock to keep me upright. I wasn't about to run a sixty yard dash, but I was walking. I'd taken a thrashing, but it could have been much worse if they'd really wanted to cripple me.

My phone buzzed in my pocket so I pulled it out. My phone screen had cracked. Damn. And I'd missed several texts from Tyson. The last was from ten minutes ago.

>>> Tired of waiting for you. Headed for the motel on foot.

I texted back. <<< Sorry. Got held up. Stay safe.

I hoped the terrain he had to cross was less perilous.

The mansion had mostly cleared out. Dead bodies could do that to a party. An ambulance had shown up in my absence and they'd somehow removed Dr. Marcus's corpse from the underfloor aquarium. The soggy body was on a stretcher and partially inserted into a body bag in the foyer. Marcus's top half was still exposed and one of the paramedics had his arm in her hands, inspecting his skin. Swain cleared the body to be moved to the hospital morgue. The paramedic drew Swain's attention to the dead doctor's arm. There was blood between two of his knuckles. A puncture wound?

One of the EMTs gave me a curious stare as she walked past. Maybe I looked like a patient too. Then I recalled she'd been one of the ones to pick up Fabienne at the dock.

Mali Solomon stood near the gurney with her arms crossed tightly. For once she was without her bevy of friends and admirers. She watched silently as the EMTs zipped up the corpse and wheeled it out the broad front doors to the drive. Our eyes met across the space formerly occupied by the body and she took in my battered face. It was enough to stir her from her contemplation.

"Luke Angel. What the hell happened to you?"

"I tripped."

"Off a cliff?"

"Sorry for your loss." I jerked my head toward the doorway. "I know he was a friend of yours."

"Why are you sorry? You have something to do with it?" Her eyes were flint. I'd seen that look plenty before. Anger always comes before acceptance on the path of grief. It was a road I'd walked enough to know.

"Any idea how he got down there?"

The lights in the living room had been dimmed, but a few still shone enough to catch the occasional glint of scales from darting fish beneath the surface of the glass. The illusion of their tropical paradise had been disturbed. A lot of that going on around here.

"There's an access grate," she said. "They think he must have accidentally fallen through."

"Or somebody pushed him in," I mused.

Mali Solomon's eyes flashed. "You know how often we've had murder on this island? Never. Doesn't happen here. Ever."

"Never is a long time."

"Julian was dealing with some personal shit. He had his problems."

"You're thinking he could have killed himself? Or are you talking about some kind of overdose?"

"I don't know what I think. But the press are gonna rip into this like sharks. I know that." Her eyes found Whitney Gilton on the back deck with her voice recorder, interviewing a trembling couple. "'Murder at Mali's.' I can already see the clickbait headlines."

"Was Marcus into anything he shouldn't have been? Something that could get him killed?"

"I told you, nobody gets killed on Sunlit Cay. It's just a quiet island."

"Your quiet island has more trouble than you give it credit for."

"Thanks to me, is that what you mean? I'm sure that's what they're going to say. Island paradise with no history of problems ever, and I show back up and look what happens. They'll come up with all that 'money corrupts' shit and say this was on me somehow."

"Seems like you're the victim to me. How are you not?"

"No rich black woman ever gets to play the victim for long. You watch. If I was a man, sure. I could play it. But when you're a successful woman, they always look for a way to cut your legs out from under you. Even the ones who cheered you on the way up. Even the women you think have your back. They've got the sharpest knives of all." She looked around. She certainly had been abandoned by the earlier hangers-on.

"Dr. Marcus was the face of your charity. You think this could have been about your work with him somehow?"

"Who could be mad about charity work? They don't think I give enough? How much else could they want?"

Mali glared at the mostly empty room. Lingering staff members spoke quietly with Swain. A few last guests whispered in an adjacent room. When she spoke again, Mali's voice had a new resignation to it. "Supporting Dr. Marcus was the best thing I ever did for this island. If somebody killed him, they're sending me a message."

"If it's a message, they sent it to everyone in this place pretty loudly."

"Tell you one thing," Mali said. "When I find them, they're gonna get a message right back they won't like. This shit won't stand. You'd better fly away quick, Luke Angel. The party on Sunlit is over." She left me to dwell on that as she moved off to rejoin her remaining guests.

Whitney Gilton found me a few minutes later.

"Oh my God, what happened to your face?" Her hand gripped my arm as she emoted over the state of my battered clothing.

But I barely heard her. I was too busy wondering who else on this island might be busy sharpening their knives.

TWENTY-THREE
DIRT

WHITNEY CLUNG to my arm while the ambulance containing Dr. Marcus's body drove away. Lingering any longer on the premises was going to draw questions, so we made our way around the back of the house to the Bronco, me moving slowly, but moving.

"Are you sure you're able to drive?" Whitney asked. She helped me get the driver's side door open, and I eased myself onto the driver's seat.

"Never better," I groaned, and got settled. My muscles had stiffened to the point where reaching for the seat belt was difficult, so Whitney did it, reaching across and buckling it for me.

"This doesn't work if we end up in a ditch."

"It's a short drive." I started the truck, then found reverse and let out the clutch slowly. Everything hurt.

As our Bronco's headlights swept across the nearly empty drive, they found the one remaining vehicle still parked behind the house, a white Lexus SUV. I stared at it as I fought the gear shift into second again, then paused.

"I've seen that car. It was outside Ruth Solomon's house this afternoon."

"Probably hers," Whitney said, double-checking the recordings on her phone.

I pulled the Bronco in front of the Lexus and studied the windshield. There was a priority parking tag hanging from the rear view mirror for The Solomon Center. Like a doctor might have.

"Might be Dr. Marcus's car," I said. "He definitely left in a different ride tonight. Makes sense why it would still be here."

"Oh. True," Whitney said, her eyes brightening. She popped her door open again and scurried out, making a quick circumnavigation of the SUV and noting the license plate. She peered in the windows briefly too, took one picture with her phone, then took a loose bunch of her dress and used it to cover her fingers while she tried the door handle.

I rolled the Bronco's window down. "Hey, what are you doing?"

"Just taking a quick peek," she said. The door was unlocked and popped open, which didn't surprise me much. Small island life. But the moment she got the door open something fell out. The ball of fabric revealed itself to be the jacket Dr. Marcus had been wearing earlier. She scooped it from the gravel, but paused when something fell out of it. She stared at the little plastic baggy and swore. "Is that what I think it is?"

The little baggy of white powder wasn't a prescription, that was obvious.

"Whitney, get back in the truck."

"Shit. What do I do with it? Do I pick it back up?"

"Leave it on the ground. Let's go."

She tossed the jacket back onto the driver's seat and gingerly closed the door. But not before taking a quick video of the interior and the little baggy on the ground.

She scurried back to the Bronco and climbed in. "You're right though. It's his car. His hospital ID was in his center console." Her eyes were wide, pupils dilated behind her stylish glasses.

She was in her element, investigative reporter mode. It was a high she was riding. "What a crazy night, huh?" She brushed a strand of loose hair away from her face. Some had come undone over the course of the evening. She looked less like a librarian now. Fire was lit inside her, adrenaline flowing.

My enthusiasm was long spent. I drove us out the gate and onto the main road, vigilant for any eyes on us.

"So Doc Marcus was a user. That's a new element. This story is turning into something so much bigger than I anticipated," she said. "I'll try to get some more interviews in the morning, see if I can follow up on that." She made a note on her phone's notes app.

"I have a mandate from Mali Solomon's security guys that I'm expected to be airborne at first light. So you might want to conduct your interviews via Zoom."

"What? No. They think they can do this to you and get away with it? Hell no. You have rights."

"Maybe you've noticed, there's not much in the way of law enforcement here. Mali's security guys hold a lot of sway. And my job is to get you home safely." I checked the rear view mirror and found it clear, so I settled my eyes on the road ahead. "Safety hasn't exactly been the theme of the night so far."

"Maybe Marcus was high tonight. Wait, you think someone took advantage of it and killed him?"

"Who just leaves their drugs sitting in an unlocked car?" I muttered.

"But who's going to mess with his car? It's a Mali Solomon party. There were probably plenty of other drugs there. Free ones. No one is going out of their way to steal his."

"I smelled some pot in the air," I said. "But that baggy was something else. Heroin maybe. A big step up."

"Not as big as you think. Could have been others there doing it too."

I thought back to my first impression of Marcus in the hospital. He'd looked undernourished for a well-paid surgeon, gaunt even. I hadn't seen it as a sign of drug use then, but that piece of the puzzle fit now. If Marcus was using, it would explain some of his look.

"I don't know if they even have a medical examiner on this island," I said. "But Marcus's body will end up at the Solomon Center. I have to imagine the staff there will at least run a blood test."

"It will show what he had in his system. I need to get that information." Whitney made another note in her phone.

"They won't be able to share private information like that."

"They'll have to tell Swain, though. Aren't you two buddies now?"

Swain would know. But I had other priorities than asking. I let the questions bounce around my head in silence for the rest of the drive to the motel. I locked the Bronco and limped my way to the stairs.

"You look absolutely terrible," Whitney said, slowing her walk to stay with me. "Are you sure you don't need a doctor?"

"I've had worse."

She stayed near my elbow on the way up the stairs, evidently worried I might topple over. I made the next floor unassisted, but it was a minuscule victory in an evening of losses.

The door to my and Tyson's room was the first we reached. I swiped the keycard and cracked the door slowly. The only light was in the area of the bathroom, but it cast enough of a glow to reveal both Tyson and Fabienne asleep in the room. They were atop the covers on separate beds, but there was something in their posture that spoke of familiarity. They were both curled facing one another, like perhaps they had fallen asleep talking.

"Why don't you get your things and come clean up in my room?" Whitney offered, eyeing the two on the beds. "That way you don't have to wake them."

There was something childlike in the faces of Fabienne and Tyson while asleep. Having first met Fabienne while unconscious, I felt like I'd barely known her awake at this point, but her expression while sleeping looked less stressed. Dreaming something hopeful perhaps. More reason not to wake her. I collected a few things and left them both to their dreams.

Whitney led me down the corridor and around the corner to her room. It faced the cove.

"That Kaleb in the office is a smooth liar," I said. "Told me there were no water views left."

"Maybe you didn't ask nicely enough." Whitney smiled and pushed her way inside.

To be fair, if I was him, I'd have given her a nicer room too.

She made straight for the sink that sat outside the bathroom and by the time I'd deposited my bag on the bureau, Whitney had warmed a washcloth and stood ready to apply it. But she took a look at my face in the better lighting of the vanity and frowned. My eye had swollen and it looked like a toddler had taken a go at my face with a purple marker.

"Geez, I don't even know where to start. They really did a number on you. Didn't you at least fight back?"

"I was assigned the role of punching bag tonight. I'll need to have a few words with the program director."

"I hope at least a few of them have bruises to match."

"Not sure about bruises, but I drained the battery on their Taser some."

Whitney blanched. "They used a Taser? Jesus."

She took a few tentative dabs at my face and hairline with the wet cloth and it came away dirty and bloody both times. I winced when she found a slice near my temple, but I did it in a manly way. Her touch was soft for the most part and I couldn't say I minded it.

"Okay, yeah. This isn't working at all," she finally said of her bloody washcloth.

She looked me over once more, then jerked her head toward the doorway to the bathroom. "It's into the shower for you."

I slipped out of my jacket and she helped pull it the rest of the way off me, tucking it over one arm afterward. "You need help with the rest?" She peered at me over the rim of her glasses.

"I'll manage."

I closed myself into the bathroom.

Her room had a larger shower than in my room. Looked inviting.

My clothes lay where they fell on the floor as I shed them, largely because I lacked the ability to bend over and pick them up. But the shower pressure was stellar and it was hot from the moment I climbed in. I just let the steaming water flow over me for a few minutes before even attempting to move. Even after the soaking, my stiff muscles still complained. My adrenaline had long since worn off and had left only a shakiness to my movements. When I reached for the complimentary bottle of body wash, my fingers weren't up to the challenge. I fumbled it and it landed with a wet thud on the tiled shower floor.

I swore.

"Are you okay in there?" Whitney called from the vicinity of the vanity.

"Fine!" I lied.

I stared at the bottle of body wash near the center floor drain and decided it was going to have to stay there. Shampoo was a perfectly reasonable substitute under the circumstances. I reached for that instead, focusing harder on the job.

But as my fingers closed on it this time, I felt a draft. The foggy glass of the shower door swung open and Whitney Gilton stood watching me. Her hair was still up but she'd removed her glasses due to all the steam in the room. All trace of buttoned-up librarian was gone now, mainly because she had nothing left on to button up. She stood nude and exposed in the doorway, my view of her long legs now revealing a lot more than just her well-defined calves.

She stepped into the shower slowly, crouching low as she did and scooping up the bottle of body wash I'd dropped. When she rose again, she had droplets of water glistening like dew in her hair and flecks of it clung to her lithe naked body.

"Decided you could use some help," she said, closing the door behind her.

"I'm feeling as helpless as they get," I confirmed, hot water still pounding against my back. "But my prognosis is improving by the minute."

"Hmm. I can see that." She cracked a smile while she opened the bottle of soap and dabbed some into a washcloth. She wet the cloth and began rubbing it over my chest and shoulders, moving in closer as she did so, the water wetting her lower half as I shifted to give her space.

"I'm doing this for purely selfish reasons. I can't have any pilot I hire looking this dirty," she clarified. Her hands moved over my chest and down my stomach. "It's a bad look for the company."

"Gotta keep that image clean," I said. "Got it."

"It's important to me." She kept up the gentle scrubbing. "But it's okay if my pilot *thinks* a little dirty from time to time. Maybe even *behaves* a little dirty? In private." She fixed me with her brilliant eyes while her hands roamed farther south. "Because I know, I do."

I steadied myself with one hand against the wall while her

hands explored me. She took my free hand and pressed it to her hip, then eased her body against mine. I ran my hand up her slick back then down till I could clench her fit, firm ass and pull her tightly against me. "Huh, it's been a long dirty day for you too then?"

Her breath was slightly ragged and our lips grazed each others' when she whispered back, "It's been an absolutely filthy day."

TWENTY-FOUR
ONE JOB

I WOKE in Whitney Gilton's bed sometime around sunrise. I was nude and sore and still vaguely exhausted. But Whitney herself was nowhere in sight. I sat up slowly and rubbed my neck. A beam of sunlight shone through a crack in the blinds and a few motes of dust danced lazily in the air. A moment later, they scattered as the bathroom door opened and Whitney emerged, hair done and fully dressed in a pencil skirt and freshly ironed blouse.

"Morning," she said brightly.

Her makeup was flawless and she bent nimbly to pick up an article of clothing from the floor. It turned out to be a pair of panties she had worn at one point last night before losing them again. She folded them neatly into her bag, then fixed both hands on her hips while appraising me. "How are we feeling this morning?"

"Top notch."

"You should hydrate. You had a tiring night."

"You don't seem any worse for wear. I'm shocked and disillusioned with myself."

"Don't be. You performed admirably. I had no expectations you were going to rally that well, or that flexibly, considering your injuries."

"I had an inspiring physical therapist."

"I'd be interested in testing your fitness again this morning, but I have work to do. You going to be okay?"

"Where are you dashing off to?"

"Journalism calls. I'm going to interview some people at the Solomon Center, see what I can dig up about Dr. Marcus's extracurriculars."

"I doubt other doctors are going to cough up dirt on one of their own. Especially if the reputation of their hospital is at stake."

"Who says I'm talking to doctors? A lot of other people work there. Nurses, medical assistants, X-ray techs. The farther down the hierarchy you go, the more complaints you'll find. Because shit rolls downhill at places like that, and not just the kind that ends up in bedpans."

"Maybe I'll come with you. I have a few questions of my own."

"You need to reunite Fabienne with the evidence she says she has. And we'll need to copy and save all of it to the cloud so when I blow this story open, our proof doesn't somehow end up under water again."

I checked the clock on the nightstand. "Not to rush your fine journalism, but we don't have a lot of time before the weather goes south. Last I checked, that tropical storm had us in its sights starting sometime today. If you want off this island before it shows up, you'd better investigate fast."

"You can't rush a good story."

"Can't slow down a hurricane either."

"Okay, I'd better get to it then," she said. "I'll call you in a bit." She moved to the door, but then thought twice and came to the bedside and cupped my face in her hands. She kissed me, her lips lingering on mine several seconds. Long enough for my hand to make it up her leg to her firm backside again.

"Work's kind of overrated," I said when the kiss ended.

"Isn't it though?" she whispered back, her forehead touching mine. But then she straightened and removed my hand from her skirt. "I've gotta go."

She pivoted and beelined for the door, and this time didn't look back.

When she was gone, I contemplated the bedsheets for a few seconds, then threw them aside. It was a stiff, slow walk to the vanity mirror for a splash in the sink. The bruises on my body were mostly purple or yellow in hue though a couple looked damned near black. My lat muscles bore a few notable fingernail scratches as well that I hadn't worn previously. Wear and tear was taking multiple forms today.

I stretched and checked my joints, then retrieved my clothing. I wasn't moving full speed, but I was still in the game.

Whitney's room boasted a view of the marina from her rear balcony so I took that in with a bottle of water in hand as I let the coffee maker percolate. The view included the docks adjoining Chuck's salvage yard. His wrecker boat was tied off to the salvage side of the marina and sitting on the adjacent shore was the recognizable form of the Cessna 182. The horizontal stabilizer had been crumpled by the lifting straps on its way up from the deep, but the red-and-white fuselage was mostly intact, as were the wings. The sight of the plane stirred my curiosity again.

I was certain the salvage boat hadn't been in the marina the night before. Must have been a late night for Chuck.

When my coffee was ready, I took it with me down the corridor to the room I shared with Tyson.

"There you are," he said when I opened the door. "'Bout damn time."

"You're up early," I said.

Fabienne was awake too. Both of them still wore the same clothes from the night before.

"The hell happened to your face?" Tyson asked, getting a better look at me.

"Long story, but not an interesting one. You two made it back safely, though, that's the main thing."

"Your friend said you can get me off this island today," Fabienne said. "We've been watching the weather and it looks bad."

The TV was on and a meteorologist was busy pointing to a spaghetti model of the tropical storm's track. It was currently projected to go straight through us and possibly strengthen to a category one hurricane by landfall. The timeline showed we'd be in the thick of it around midnight.

"We'll leave today. It'll be bumpy, but nothing *Tropic Angel* can't handle. If we pick our headings right, we might even have a nice tailwind for the ride."

Tyson and Fabienne looked reassured. I strode across the room and located my toothbrush.

"I still need to talk to the reporter," Fabienne said. "Dr. Marcus needs to be exposed. He's gotten away with too much already. I came this far and I'm not leaving till I know we're bringing him down."

"You haven't heard then. Dr. Marcus is dead." I watched her face carefully as I said it.

"Dead?" The way her eyes widened appeared authentic. That or she was a great actress.

It took me five minutes to catch them up on the rest of the night at Mali Solomon's, delayed somewhat by my intermittent teeth brushing, but when I was done with both, Fabienne looked anything but satisfied. She looked pissed off.

"He's not supposed to be dead. He's supposed to pay for what he did."

"Might argue he did?" Tyson suggested. "Dude's kicked off."

"At a party? Getting high? That's not punishment. That's the easy way out. My father suffered from what that man did. He lost his life in pain."

I put up my toothbrush and dried my face. "Much as you might want vengeance on Marcus, it's not how this one played out. You're going to have to find a way to get peace with your father's death another way."

"Oh, it's that easy? I've spent months getting to the bottom of this. I gave up school for it. This isn't how it's supposed to end. Him not even being held accountable? Never paying for it?"

"I've lost a parent too. I know some of what you're feeling right now. It doesn't always get tied up neatly for the people they leave behind. Sometimes raw stays raw for a long time."

"Was your parent murdered by a merciless psychopath that everyone idolizes?"

"No. She was killed by the father I used to idolize. But we're not playing 'Whose Parents Got Killed Worse?' here. It's not going to fix anything."

"Well, I'm sorry you gave up on your mother's memory, but I'm not giving up yet. My father died at the hands of Dr. Marcus, and Marcus didn't do it alone. He was sponsored and encouraged. He had Mali Solomon bankrolling his killings and she needs to go down too."

"I get your fervor here, but Mali Solomon is a famous game designer and millionaire. What possible motive would she have to finance an illegal organ smuggling operation?"

"Because she's evil and if you knew her, I bet you would see it."

"I did talk to her last night, and as much as I feel your pain on this, I think it's possible you're letting your emotions steer you into seeing something that might not be there."

"So what, you're on her side now? And I'm just being *emotional*?"

"That's not what I'm trying to—"

"That's fine. I'll get the evidence myself. I thought you two were going to help me, but if I have to keep doing everything on my own, I will." She dug into the drawer next to the nightstand and pulled out the .22 handgun she'd stashed and stuffed it into the back of her pants. "And I'll get off this damned island myself too. Thanks for nothing," she said to Tyson, and stormed out the door.

"Fabienne, wait," Tyson said, following her out. "He ain't really mean all that." He disappeared after her down the corridor, but a few moments later, reappeared. He held both palms up in my direction. "Dude. Seriously? We just finally found this girl."

"I know."

"Emotional? You had to know that was gonna tick her off. You can't say shit like that these days. Even *I* know that one. You gonna blame the whole thing on PMS next?"

"Probably get us shot."

"Pfft. You'd deserve it, too. You gotta get with the times, man. Girls don't tolerate that shit. And you're supposed to be the smooth talking one."

"Nobody bats a thousand."

"Big swing and a miss for sure. Whiffed so hard the wind blew my hair back. And I ain't even got the hair for that."

"I'll make it up to her."

"How? She ran off."

"Go find her. She still needs her bag back. And she still needs to meet with Whitney."

"You and that reporter girl on a first name basis now? Where she at, anyway?"

"Still investigating." I tossed my empty coffee cup in the trash and took another look at the map the weather forecaster still had up. I found the remote and turned the TV off. "Catch up to Fabienne before she gets too far. I'll gather our stuff and check out of this place. These women can have an hour or two, but once we get them wrangled back to the airport, we'll get out of here."

"Uh, they don't seem the type to like being *wrangled*."

"Then we'll politely *invite* them back to the plane and get the hell out of here. The last thing any of us need is to be sitting on this tiny island while it's being pummeled by a cat one hurricane. They may have other plans today, but we have one job."

"Get our passengers home safely."

"Exactly."

Tyson gave me a nod, then rushed back out the door to find Fabienne.

I carefully gathered our remaining things and closed the door behind us.

One job. Simple.

But this one job was starting to get on my nerves.

TWENTY-FIVE
STINGER

I'D JUST TOSSED our bags into the back of the rental Bronco when I spotted Constable Swain leaving the neighboring salvage yard. He had his deputy with him, the woman I'd met the previous night. He caught my eye so I gave him a wave. It was good to see the investigation of the downed plane was still proceeding despite the chaos of the night before. Swain's deputy was checking images on her camera as they walked.

I closed the hatch of the Bronco and picked my way across the litter of palm fronds in the parking lot and made my way toward the police SUV. The gusting wind had done a good job of tree cleaning thus far, but it was just the warmup. The sky already showed the telltale signs of a rain band on the horizon and I knew the day would only get blusterier.

"We have quite a lot on our plate this morning, Mr. Angel," Swain said by way of greeting as I approached.

"On my way out anyway," I said. "Looks like Chuck found your missing plane for you, so my value to the investigation is diminishing."

"You may have met Miss Thorpe?" He gestured toward his deputy. She gave me a nod.

"Anything conclusive on the plane?" I asked.

"It's as we suspected," Swain said. "The cabin heater on the muffler. Evidence of a leak into the cockpit. One of Chuck's men was kind enough to point out several discrepancies that coincided with the leak into the interior. I'll make a report when the Air Accident Investigation Authority gets involved, but it seems conclusive. An accident. Though you were proven somewhat incorrect in your memory."

"How's that?"

"The condition of the aircraft's exhaust was far from shiny. Frankly surprised it was still in service. Perhaps your view of it under the water was a factor."

I rested my hands on my hips and inclined my head toward the deputy's camera. "Mind if I see a photo?"

Deputy Thorpe found a photo on her camera and tilted the display screen toward me. The photo did indeed show a corroded exhaust system. The stacks and muffler were in rough shape. A hole was worn in the muffler shroud dead center, in the area where it would have passed above the carb air box.

"Huh," I muttered. "Sure enough."

"I wouldn't feel badly about it," Swain added. "The amount of times I've interviewed witnesses after an event and received inaccurate accounts of colors or descriptions is beyond counting. Especially in poor light. During academy training I once interviewed a woman who had been mugged and she entirely failed to notice the man had only been wearing a Speedo." He pulled his sunglasses off and appraised my face. "At least it seems you are mostly recovered from your incident last night. I put together a report on it and will have words with the director of security for Solomon's estate."

"I didn't ask you to do that."

"I won't abide violence on this island, Mr. Angel. We're a small community and our reputation is everything to us."

"How will your little island's reputation fair without Dr. Marcus around?"

Swain's expression darkened. "Another blight we will have to deal with. But Julian Marcus did far more good than harm on this island. His death is tragic but also an apparent accident."

"What kind of harm?" I pressed.

His mouth formed a firm line. "The accidental death of Dr. Marcus is not an investigation you are a part of, Mr. Angel. Your assistance in that area won't be required."

I put up my hands. "I'll stay out of it."

Swain nodded and he and Thorpe turned toward his vehicle.

"Won't even tell anyone it was drug related," I added.

Swain pulled his door open, but paused and turned back, studying me. His brow pinched. "You're fishing."

"Am I?"

"What concern is it of yours?"

"Aren't we all concerned? Reputation of the island and all that?"

"You're not an islander, Mr. Angel. You don't owe Sunlit Cay any more of your time."

"You're probably right. Don't need any more of my faulty memories clouding up your investigations."

He gave me a long stare, but then climbed into his SUV and shut the door. The vehicle backed out and drove away, and I was left standing in the parking lot. I studied the corroded tin gate to the salvage yard and frowned.

I walked back to the Bronco and climbed in. I had passengers to pick up. I started the Bronco, but when I put my arm over the back of the seat to look behind me, I paused. Swain's comment niggled at me.

I put the truck back in neutral, pulled out my phone and made a call.

Reese Winter picked up on the third ring.

"Better late than never?"

"That's becoming my new motto."

"On your way back then? Your dog is starting to mope."

"Tell him I'll be home soon. You in the office by chance?"

"Have my feet up on your desk. Figured I'd cash your paycheck too since you don't seem to work here anymore."

"Do me a favor. Look up the registration number of that 182 on the FAA registry."

"The wrecked one? What's the tail number?"

"November Seven Six One Mike."

She typed the registration number loudly enough to hear the keystrokes. "Cessna 182 M. Got it. Registered to a Cloud-Hopper Aviation in Fort Lauderdale. What do you want now?"

"Engine model."

"Says Continental O-520."

"That's an upgrade. Bet it came with an O-470."

"Nice boost in horsepower, but why do we care?"

"You remember last year working on Doc Callahan's 182? We put that bigger engine on. He went with the IO-520."

"Sure."

"Can you see if you can find me a parts list with the invoice?"

"What are you after?"

"Pretty sure that we did an exhaust upgrade with it."

"Had to. You ram all that extra exhaust volume though the original diameter exhaust system, it makes for failures. Back pressure issues too."

"If you find the parts list, will you text me a picture?"

"Sure. Anything else?"

I mused out the windshield. "Yeah. See if you can find who did the maintenance on the downed plane. Odds are they know the plane went down and are prepping for an investigation anyway, so they might be guarded, especially with a fatality involved, but see if you can talk to whoever was doing the work. Check when the engine conversion was done and if they upgraded the exhaust system with it."

"You got it."

"Thanks, Reese."

"You kicking hornets' nests over there? You have that tone of voice you get when you're about to get into something sticky."

"Only poking a little."

"You know you're not supposed to pick fights without me."

"I always like you in my corner, but I should be fine."

"All right, but if you don't come back soon, I'm keeping your dog."

"Murphy does appreciate that your house doesn't float."

"Hey, Luke?"

"Yeah."

"Don't get stung."

TWENTY-SIX
HOLDING PATTERN

FABIENNE HADN'T GOT FAR. I spotted her and Tyson talking on the stretch of beach adjoining The Boneyard.

I parked the Bronco in a space at the side of the restaurant and squinted in the wind when I got out.

Kate, the girl we'd had for a bartender the first night, was on the front deck of the restaurant stowing patio umbrellas and closing shutters. She gave me a wave.

"Closing early today?" I asked as I walked up.

"Kitchen is open for takeout for the next hour, but after that we're done."

The bar's awnings were already down and lashed shut and the restaurant was vacant.

"Been through a few of these before, I take it."

She looked around the grounds. "Nothing like working in a place filled with sharp rusty objects in a windstorm, huh?"

"Coconut Chuck around?"

"Not yet. He had a late night. He and the guys didn't get back till early this morning with that plane. Probably still asleep." The marina had mostly cleared out. Chuck's wrecker sat at anchor out in the cove. Only its shore boat was still at the dock, but lifted from the water by a hoist. Looked to be a bay boat with a single Yamaha outboard on the back.

"He live close by?"

"That's his place there."

She pointed to a bungalow on stilts that sat on the bluff on the far side of the little stretch of beach Tyson was on. "Don't think you'll see him this morning though. And he doesn't really like visitors coming up to his place."

"Sees enough of people at the bar."

She nodded. "You getting out today? Hate to see that pretty old plane of yours get all beat up in the wind."

"Soon. Just gathering up my passengers." I gestured down the beach toward Fabienne and Tyson.

"Take good care of yourselves. Gonna be rough today." She took a loose wooden sign off the facade of the building, clutched it to her chest, then disappeared indoors with it.

Once she was gone, I trudged across the little stretch of private beach to where Fabienne and Tyson sat on the hull of an overturned wooden rowboat. Looked like it had been there a while. Victim of a prior storm? Fabienne's glare as I walked up wasn't friendly, but had an air of resignation to it.

"I apologize," I said. "I was out of line."

She had her arms crossed, but slowly unclenched her white-knuckled hold on her elbows and exhaled. "You still have my stuff."

"Let's go get it."

"I don't care if you think I'm crazy. I'm not."

"I don't think you're crazy. You've worked hard to get this far. Let's go see this thing as far as we can with the time we've got."

She studied my face another long moment, then pushed off the hull of the boat and stood. Then she started back toward the truck, her feet kicking up sand behind her.

"You gonna help her now?" Tyson asked.

"I'm always a helpful guy." I checked my watch. "For limited windows of time."

"That apology seemed to work. You just came right out with that, huh?"

"A man shouldn't be afraid to admit his mistakes. If you can't acknowledge you've got room for improvement, you'll never improve."

"Tell that to my dad. He ran out on my mom ten years ago, and I don't think he's said sorry once. Always made me mad. She deserved one hell of an apology after all he put her through."

"He owes you one too."

"Yeah. I think he does," Tyson said.

I rested a hand on his shoulder. "Good thing we don't have to become like our fathers."

"Room for improvement."

"Always."

He nodded and started off after Fabienne.

I looked up at the bungalow on the bluff. The windows of the place were still open and the curtains blew in the breeze. I guess Chuck slept just fine through stormy weather. Must be nice.

I started the Bronco back up once we were all in and made our way to the airfield. The windsock stood nearly straight out, but it was still blowing mostly down the runway. I checked my phone for text messages from Whitney and found none so I sent one of my own.

>>> Paging all passengers bound for Florida. Your flight is boarding.

As soon as I had the hatch open and the ladder deployed, Tyson scooted forward to the flight deck and retrieved Fabienne's satchel from where I'd stashed it in the tunnel to the bow.

Fabienne climbed aboard and took a tentative look around the interior of *Tropic Angel*.

"This thing flies?"

"It's a restoration project," I replied, climbing up the ladder behind her. "For a plane from the 1940s, this interior is charming."

"If you say so." She moved tentatively up the cabin to the passenger area.

Owing to the cargo payload on the way over, I had the Mallard configured with only four of the passenger seats it could usually hold. But the fact I didn't own many more seats contributed as well. Planes previously used for careers in the drug smuggling business didn't always have the best accessories. But this Mallard still had a decent headliner and side panels. The coat closet and lavatory were still usable too. The waterproof carpeted floor panels needed a good cleaning, but active seaplanes weren't known for pretty flooring.

Tyson handed Fabienne her satchel and she flung the top open with vigor, quickly scanning the contents. She pulled files from their folders and rifled through them, but her enthusiasm quickly turned to swearing.

"These signatures all got ruined." She flipped through file after file, but her expression grew more morose with each one. "I need to be able to prove Marcus and his people signed off on these procedures or none of this will stick."

"Those are your proof?" I asked.

She fanned a few of the files out on the adjacent seat. "These are legit donors. Legal organs from mostly the US. And these are recipients, patients who received the donated organs. It's all anonymous donation, but you'll see that the code up here in the file matches the donor file."

"What's wrong with that?" I asked.

"Nothing." She slid another file on top of the one I was looking at. "Except when it happens twice. Here is another recipient. Look at the code."

"It's the same code. So same donor? Still not impossible, right? Multiple organs from the same donor?"

Fabienne pointed to the two recipient patient files. "Lungs or kidneys, sure. But how many donors do you know who can give two livers?"

I read the surgery descriptions. "Shit. You're right."

"One of these livers came from someone else," Fabienne said. "Here's another donor who would have to have given three kidneys." She reached into the blue files and came up with a piece of paper. "Now this." She handed it to me. "Missing person report."

"I can't read Haitian Creole."

"Just look at the date."

The woman was listed as missing the day before the third kidney transplant.

"And how long is the window for a kidney transplant?" I asked, already sure what I'd hear.

"Twenty-four to forty-eight hours. But livers are eight to twelve." She handed me one of the files from a liver transplant recipient and the missing person report. They'd happened on the same day.

"I'm sorry I didn't believe you," I said.

"It's okay. I probably wouldn't have believed me either. But without the signatures from Marcus, I don't know if it's enough to stick."

"Your passports still work," I said. "You get out of here, tell your story to Whitney and the Herald, and see what she can do with it from the US. If this thing is as corrupt as you think, there's more evidence to be found."

"With Julian Marcus dead, then this whole thing will get buried with him. You think Mali Solomon will leave evidence to be found by the police? If I don't have solid evidence now, the Herald will never print anything." She dug around in the bag and came out with the flash drive. She held it in her hand then clutched it to her chest. "Oh thank God."

"Backups?" I asked.

"It's not the originals, but at least they'll be legible. And date stamped. And it has the plane video. Maybe that's enough?"

Tyson scratched at his head. "Not to be a downer but that thing's been in the ocean. 'Less you got a big bag of rice to stick it in for a month, I don't know if it's gonna work."

Fabienne checked the end of the drive and brushed a few flecks of salt from the USB connector. "It has to work."

"There was a cafe up the road," Tyson suggested. Maybe someone got a laptop we can try it in?"

"Whitney has a laptop," I said. "She can check it as soon as she gets herself here." I pulled out my phone again and moved to the doorway. "She said she was getting poor reception though. We may have to go find her."

The windsock on the pole was whipping side to side in the gusts and seemed to be shifting more toward a crosswind.

"Let's get some of the preflight checklist done and I'll file our flight plan. If we haven't heard from Whitney by the time that's done, we'll go get her."

The Mallard's preflight checks were a pretty standard pulling of inlet covers and flight control checks, but I put the control locks back in again afterward due to the wind. Tyson and I pulled each of the propellers through by hand a few times to check for hydraulic lock in the cylinders of the big radial engines.

"Luke?" Tyson called from the left engine. "Is this a problem?"

I walked over and found him on the step stool struggling to move the big prop. "Won't budge past here."

"Yeah. That's what I was worried about. That lowest plug was oily last time I cleaned it too. We'll have to pull it and drain that oil out of the cylinder. Probably just the bottom one."

"What's the matter?" Fabienne climbed down the boarding ladder. "Is it broken?"

"Just needs a little TLC. These old engines can pool oil in the lower cylinders and create a fluid blockage. You have to be careful you don't bend a connecting rod or damage a piston."

"Is that what happened?"

"Not yet. Because we're careful. But we'll need to fix it before we go. Don't worry, it won't take long."

"I can handle it," Tyson said, adding a wink to Fabienne. "Planes are my thing."

"Get started and I'll finish the rest of the preflight."

By the time I'd checked fuel and oil quantity and was satisfied with the plane's general readiness, there was still no word back from Whitney.

Fabienne was watching Tyson gather tools and he seemed to be relishing the attention.

"I'm going to go find Whitney," I said. "You got this?"

"No problem. This is easy stuff."

"You two stay out of trouble."

"Should I come with you?" Fabienne said.

"You're in good hands. Hoping I won't be long."

I took the Bronco back to the Solomon Center. The same friendly guy I'd met the first time was behind the counter but he'd donned a black armband of mourning over his jacket sleeve—something I hadn't seen done in years—and his previous megawatt smile was missing.

"I'm looking for a woman named Whitney Gilton," I said and showed him her photo. "Came in this morning. Have you seen her?"

"Yes, sir. But you just missed her. She left not ten minutes ago."

"On foot?"

"No sir, she had a ride. Called herself a taxi."

"Tell me she was headed for the airport."

"No. Afraid not, sir. She asked me for an address south of here that I didn't actually have. Said she was headed to the old Solomon place."

"Mali Solomon's mansion?"

"Oh no, sir. That would have been easy to find. She wanted the old house. It's back on the beach south of the current estate. The one Dr. Marcus owned."

"Dr. Marcus owned the house the Solomons lived in?"

"Long time ago. Miss Mali grew up in it. Nobody's lived there for a long time now though from what I hear."

"Any idea why Whitney—Miss Gilton, was headed there?"

"No, sir. She didn't say."

I took the same vague directions he'd given her, then thanked him.

I called Tyson's phone from the truck but Fabienne picked up.

"You two okay?" I asked.

"Your friend is oily and didn't want to touch his phone."

"I'm taking a detour." I told her where Whitney had gone.

"Told you Marcus and the Solomons go way back. All of this ties them together."

Small islands are usually tightly knit communities. It didn't surprise me I was finding more connections. But I had to wonder what might unravel if I pulled too hard on the knots.

I was about to find out.

TWENTY-SEVEN
THE OLD HOUSE

THE BRONCO HAD a significant advantage in speed over the golf cart I'd rented previously, not to mention the ability to take the lumps and holes I found myself bumping my way over after I left the paved road.

I missed the turn twice, but finally located it. The track I found myself on was overgrown, but not so much as to be impassable. It had obviously seen enough traffic to keep the grass out of the ruts, but just barely. Except the farther down the road I went, the worse the road got. A half mile in, I found a gray sedan idling at the side of the track, the driver still behind the wheel. I rolled down the passenger window and peered across. The sedan driver had his window down too.

"Are you the cab?"

"Uber." He pointed up the road. "Waiting. She went up on foot."

"I'll probably be her ride back. But wait if you want."

"Meter's running," he said, indicating the phone on his dash. "Unless she tells me otherwise."

The Bronco's higher ground clearance gave it the ability to

roll on, so I did. It was another eighth of a mile or so when I saw the house. It was the white, boarded-up house Tyson and I had overflown from the air.

Had it not been for the run-down state of the place, the property would be beautiful. The house sat nearly on the beach, palms waving in the breeze. What might have once been a patch of lawn was now overrun with sand and dune grass. The sand was actually so thick in places, it piled up against the house like snow drifts.

And it was pink.

There was an old truck parked next to the house and I recognized that too.

I climbed out of the Bronco and approached the dilapidated porch. A few scraps of yellowed paint still peeled from the porch railing. The door was a faded blue. I knocked, and waited.

When the door opened, Mama Jacqui stood in the doorway with a resigned expression on her face. "Figured you might show up. Come on in. Your friend is already here."

I entered what once might have been a person's livable home. Now the floor was littered with leaves and tracked-in sand. A fat palmetto bug scurried into a corner behind a moth eaten armchair in the living room, but looked at home there.

Mama Jacqui gestured me onward toward the kitchen where I found Whitney Gilton browsing a dusty shelf of picture frames.

"Must be the day for questions," Mama Jacqui said. "I assume you two know each other."

Whitney gave me a smile. "We've met."

Mama Jacqui sized us up, her shrewd eyes assessing me longest. "Seems like you have a habit of following the pretty young women around this island."

"One way to put it."

"How would you enjoy it if you were the follow-ee?"

"Having someone else concerned for my safety? I wouldn't mind."

"I'm concerned for your safety. After that stunt you pulled yesterday with the plane, I think you brought yourself some unwanted attention."

"Isn't that the game these days? Attention at all costs? Promote yourself or die. Am I not doing it right?"

"Most people want to stay on the good side of Mali Solomon. And her friends," Mama Jacqui said. "You seem to be antagonizing everybody."

"Dr. Marcus was on her good side. How did that work out for him?"

Mama Jacqui's head bobbed slowly and she shuffled over to a dingy chair at a dining room table littered with moldy cardboard boxes. She sank into the chair with a defeated sigh. She gestured to the room at large. "All the work he did, and this is the legacy he leaves behind for us."

"Could do with a maid service."

"He didn't often come here in the mood to clean. I'd find him here though, and do what I could to get him back on his feet."

I picked up a framed newspaper clipping from the pile. The article showed a young Mali Solomon handing an oversized check to Julian Marcus at the start of their charitable foundation. Another was of Mali and her mother Ruth at an event celebrating Mali's philanthropy.

"How do you fit into all this?" I asked. "You're cleaning up the mess?"

"I've always been there to help Julian," she replied. "Part of my job."

"We know he abused drugs," Whitney interjected. "His problem seems to be a poorly kept secret. Especially now, with his death. I spoke to the hospital staff this morning and the word is he suffered a heroin overdose."

"Julian struggled. Just like a lot of people on this island. But lately he'd been making great strides. He'd actually been clean for several months up until yesterday, and seeing the benefits of his sobriety. I thought he had a real chance this time."

"You treated him?" Whitney asked.

"Even doctors need help from someone."

"Were you out here the morning I met you? Helping?"

"That's my business."

"This place doesn't look like the home of a sober man," I said.

"This wasn't his home. This was where he came when he was low. When his demons haunted him. I'd hoped he was done with this place. He told me he was leaving. Getting off Sunlit Cay for good. And I really thought he'd make it. So I came this morning, searching for clues to his misfortune, same as you."

"I looked up the address history," Whitney said. "I know Ruth and Mali Solomon used to live here. Their relationship with Dr. Marcus ran back a long way."

"Julian rented this place to Ruth Solomon because he took pity on her. It's a small island," Mama Jacqui said by way of explanation. "All the relationships here get tied to one another over time. But some more than others. That's them on the shelf there." She gestured toward the frames in front of Whitney.

Whitney pulled a picture down that was faded and worn, but depicted four youths, arms draped over one another's shoulders, smiling.

"That's Dr. Marcus?" Whitney said in awe. "So young. Wow. Ruth was a beauty."

"Didn't have to tell me that," Mama Jacqui said. "That's me on the end. Guess which one of us had the attention of the boys."

Whitney handed me the photo. The girl in the picture had the same rounded face and kind eyes as the woman sitting across from me, but some forty years separating them. She was an attractive young girl, but Ruth Solomon was in another league. Movie star looks.

"Who's the other boy?" I asked, trying to place the face.

"That's Edwin."

"Constable Swain?" I studied the photo with renewed interest. "You were all in school together?"

"Ruth and I were a grade behind the boys. But it was an all age school on a small island. Everyone was friends with everyone then."

"And now?" Whitney asked.

Mama Jacqui appraised her cautiously. "Some closer than others."

"Small island life," I said. "Someone has to be the island's memory." I set the framed photo down and took a seat opposite her. "Keep it all straight."

"Why?" she said. "So a pair of outsiders can come unravel the knots, and shine a light on all of our citizen's indiscretions? Our island may seem quaint to you, Mr. Angel, or you, Miss Gilton, but we've endured a long time. And we are not under obligation to share how with outsiders."

"There is at least one person on this island who thinks Dr. Marcus's secrets are worth digging up," Whitney said. "Someone who is owed an explanation."

"That Haitian girl, you mean. Yes, I thought this might involve her."

Whitney pulled a chair out from beside Mama Jacqui and sat. She set her phone on the table too. I noticed it was recording. "Fabienne Thompson believes Dr. Marcus was responsible for her father's death. Do you have any information about what happened to him?"

Mama Jacqui stared at the phone, then looked Whitney in the eyes. "Your Miss Thompson came to me a few days ago with the same question. I'll tell you what I told her. Julian Marcus was a man who struggled with his demons. But I have never seen or heard of him treating patients from Haiti on this island. His mission work there was an outreach he performed out of generosity through his and Mali Solomon's foundation. Though I know it pained him not to be able to do more."

I looked around the old house, unnaturally dark with its boarded-up windows.

"If saving Ruth Solomon was an act of generosity, then Mali Solomon paying him back with generosity and teaming up with him should have been a good thing, shouldn't it? Why board up the memory of his good deed and use it as the place to harbor his demons?"

Mama Jacqui's intense gaze seemed to falter on that. Her eyes narrowed in thought. "Julian told me once that saving Ruth Solomon's life wasn't an act of generosity for him. It was an offering."

"Strange way to speak of saving someone's life," Whitney said.

"Julian was deeply in love with Ruth. Before she went away. And after, when she came home with a child and an illness. I don't think there was anything he wouldn't do for her."

"An offering is a sacrifice," I said. "What did it cost him?"

Mama Jacqui pushed herself up from the chair and steadied herself with a hand on the table. "Being old and having lived here a long time grants me privileges. But I'm not omniscient. I'm just tired. Tired of seeing the demons win." She moved to the kitchen and rinsed out a glass, then filled it with water from the tap.

"I take it you've lost others to the drug problem on the island?" I asked.

"Too many."

"What about Vaughn, the lobster traps guy? He's been on my

ass like a barnacle since I got here. How does he fit into your island's history of demons?"

She shuffled back around from the sink to face us. "Vaughn Jefferson isn't from Sunlit. He's an American. Though he has been here a long time and has adopted some of the accent. Makes him feel like a local. You aren't alone in your suspicions of him."

"I'm no rocket surgeon, but if you want to get drugs to an island, you need a boat or plane and a good reason to be coming and going all over for deliveries. Lobster trapping might make a decent cover if I was looking to diversify my income sources. Becoming chief of security on an island without a lot of security wouldn't hurt either."

"You're more observant than I gave you credit for, Mr. Angel. You'll find an ally in Constable Swain with that suspicion, and he's been looking into it much longer than you have." She took a drink from her glass.

"I come from a disreputable family. You get so you recognize the tells."

"Then you understand the dangers associated with the business. And the difficulty in rooting it out of a community like Pelican Roost when it's become addicted to it."

"What I don't get is why Vaughn Jefferson would have known to hassle me right after coming to see you yesterday morning. I went looking for Fabienne and he was on me from the word go."

Mama Jacqui leaned against the kitchen countertop and narrowed her eyes at me again.

"There's a truck motor idling outside," I said. "Heard it pull up a minute ago. You text him when I got here?"

Whitney stood and collected her phone, then moved toward the door. "He's out there right now?"

"Vaughn has plenty of ways to know where you are," the old woman said. "Didn't require any help from me."

I got out of my chair.

"Vaughn Jefferson isn't a man you want to be on the wrong side of," Mama Jacqui said.

"Neither am I." I opened the door and went to meet him.

TWENTY-EIGHT
VAUGHN

VAUGHN JEFFERSON HAD PARKED his truck behind the Bronco, blocking me in.

He was alone.

It was just as well. What we had to say to each other didn't need an audience.

He was leaning against the fender of the Bronco, waiting.

"For a pilot, you got a shitty sense of direction," he said. "This look like an airport to you?"

Whitney came out onto the porch behind me, listening.

"Just gathering my passengers," I said. "We're on our way back to the airport now as a matter of fact. Pity you had to waste a trip out."

"Kind of thing I have to do all the time. Escort people out of places they have no business being."

I leaned against one of the porch supports. "We were just talking about your business inside. Seems you're a man in high demand."

"You don't know the half of it."

"Can't fault a man for having interests. But some of your

hobbies have me curious. That beach meeting we had, for example. You wanted that satchel bad enough to have your young buddy bring a baseball bat along for the acquisition. How come it was so important to you?"

"Some business deals take a few tries to iron out. We're gonna sort that deal soon. You can give it to me when we get back to the airport. 'Less you have it with you now."

"We still don't have a lot of interest in that deal."

"Because you aren't seeing all the pros and cons." His hand came out from behind his back holding a pistol. Looked like a Beretta M9. He pointed it at Whitney.

She froze.

"Vaughn. You better think real hard about your choices out here." Mama Jacqui appeared on the porch behind me.

"Hey there, Mama Jacqui. You don't have to worry about me. I'm just taking out the trash."

"This young lady is a reporter from Miami. Don't think you want to give her a bad impression of our island," Mama Jacqui said.

"Too late," Whitney muttered.

"We just need some time to get to know each other." Vaughn's eyes didn't leave Whitney. "And I have just the solution for that. You're gonna ride with me, girl."

"I have an Uber," Whitney replied.

"Carlos? Nah. I told him to split. He works for me. He made sure to tell me you were here, though."

"Told you," Mama Jacqui said to me under her breath.

"That looks like a service pistol I used to have," I said. "You serve in the army, Vaughn?"

"Did my piece. Why, you thinking maybe I'm gonna get all teary-eyed bringing up old times? I know you're ex-army too. But you and me are a long way from those days. And I ain't ever served with you."

"Just like to know what kind of man I'm dealing with."

"I think you already know. Blondie, you come on and get in the truck." He waved the pistol.

Whitney looked at me.

If it was me alone, I'd take my chances against the gun. A hard sprint would make me a tough target, and I'd outpace this guy fast enough in just about any direction. But Whitney wasn't in running shoes and if I rushed Vaughn to buy her time, there was no telling where the bullets would fly.

"Let's do as he says." I brushed her arm. "We're leaving anyway."

She looked none-too-pleased about the prospect, but made her way to Vaughn's truck.

"You drive," he said, handing her the keys. "You can be my chauffeur." He then waved the gun in my direction. "We'll pull back and let you out. Expect you to head straight to the airport, slow enough to stick together."

"Hard to get lost on this island."

"Gimme your phone."

I pulled it from my pocket and tossed it to him.

"Mama Jacqui, I'll be seeing you," Vaughn said. "Don't want to hear you been making any calls either."

Mama Jacqui watched stone-faced from the porch but didn't reply.

"Okay, we straight. Let's go," Vaughn said.

I climbed into the Bronco and led the way out, twisting down the rutted drive.

Whitney and Vaughn stuck close behind.

I checked the rear-view frequently once we got onto the main road. Vaughn was talking, one arm dropped across the seat behind Whitney's head, but she kept her eyes on the Bronco.

Scenarios ran through my head, options for how to play this, but none of them ended well. If I'd been armed, it would be a different story, but for now I had to wait for a better opening.

Vaughn seemed to be playing by the rules so far, and if us getting off the island was all he needed, that was an easy hit to take. We were leaving anyway. As much as I wanted to see Fabienne get her answers and Whitney score her story, they were both goals that could be easily sacrificed in the interest of getting out of gun range.

Live to fight another day.

I'd done evac for enough troops during my career to know the battle wasn't always won in a day.

So I'd be patient.

But when we pulled into the airport grounds, I had my first hint that things might not be that simple.

Tools were still scattered beneath the Mallard's left engine, a bucket and stepladder nearby, but no sign of Tyson or Fabienne. I pulled up to the airport gate and pressed the button for the intercom.

Basil's voice came over the speaker. "Welcome back, sir." And the gate buzzed and started rolling.

I pulled through to the ramp and put the Bronco in a rental car space next to the FBO.

Whitney parked Vaughn's truck beside me. "What's wrong with your plane?" he asked as we climbed out. The wind was gusting hard and made the Bahamian flag whip and crack above the FBO building.

"Just a little maintenance," I said. But I was wondering myself. This should have been an easy job for Tyson, well finished by now.

Vaughn tucked his pistol into the waistband of his pants, but conspicuously kept his hand on it, tucked up under his shirt. He kept his other hand on Whitney's elbow as we walked toward the plane. She tried to pull away from him, but he jerked her back close.

"Looks like maybe you're flying out on one engine," he said. "I don't give a shit how you go."

"I need to find my copilot first." The boarding door was still open. The flight deck windows too.

I climbed the boarding ladder and stuck my head in.

Fabienne was crouched inside, her back against the wall of the fuselage, the 0.22 pistol in her hand. Our eyes met for a meaningful instant, but I looked away.

"There's no one in here," I shouted back to Vaughn, and I climbed back down the ladder.

"Your boy lost?" Vaughn pulled my phone from his pocket and tossed it to me. "Call him. Keep it short."

I pressed Tyson's number on my contacts page and put the phone to my ear. As the phone rang, Whitney tensed slightly. Her eyes had been on the plane. Fabienne's face was visible for an instant in the port side window but vanished again. I gave Whitney the slightest shake of my head, but she was already on the same page. She turned away and studied the distant horizon.

The phone went to voicemail.

I swore, but I checked my texts and found one from Tyson.

"Text says he dropped a spark plug. Went to find another one."

"Spark plug? Couldn't he just pick that shit back up?"

Giving Vaughn an explanation of the danger of cracked spark plug insulators wasn't high on my priorities list, so I let the comment pass. "I'm guessing he went to Chuck's place. Unless there's someone else around here dealing in airplane parts."

Vaughn glanced in the direction of the salvage yard. "Then I guess we all going to see Chuck." He turned Whitney around and shoved her toward the truck. "You first, princess."

"Get your hands off me," she retorted.

While Vaughn was distracted with her, I glanced back at the plane. Fabienne watched us out the window, and I gestured for her to hold there.

Vaughn still hadn't reclaimed my phone yet, and I noticed I had a text from Reese too with the info I'd requested. I read quickly.

>>> We put a Powerflow exhaust upgrade on Callahan's 182.

She'd attached a photo of the parts list like I'd asked.

>>> Also called the shop in Ft. Lauderdale that did the work on N761M. They used an Air Power version of the same thing.

I was about to return a text to her when Vaughn stuck his pistol in my face. "That's enough of that, flyboy." He held his hand out for the phone.

"We've already agreed to fly out," I said. "You can stop waving that thing around."

"You seem the kind of motherfucker likes to change his mind," Vaughn said. "This here is a helpful reminder to not."

I handed him the phone. "You're the boss, boss."

That seemed to placate him. He was clearly used to everyone listening to him on this island. I felt the urge to change that. But as much as I wanted to get that gun away from him and thrash him with it, the opportunity hadn't presented itself. Plus I wasn't completely sure what Vaughn was capable of yet. Drug dealing, sure. But if what Mama Jacqui had said about Julian Marcus getting clean had been true, the drugs we'd found in the doctor's car didn't make much sense. He could have relapsed, but could they have been left to tell a different story? If so, who had better means and opportunity to plant it there than Vaughn?

He'd had time to lay into me that night with his buddies. But had he had time to kill Julian Marcus as well?

I got into the driver's seat of the Bronco again, Whitney in the passenger seat, and Vaughn in the second row with his gun.

I had no idea how he planned to deal with three of us once

we had Tyson, but we'd cross that bridge when we came to it. I shifted into gear and pulled back out of the gate. As I rested my hand on the seat next to me, Whitney's fingers interlaced with mine and I gave her hand a squeeze before having to release it to shift again. It wasn't much, but it was something to reassure her. We were in this together now.

But as we pulled away and *Tropic Angel* faded into the rearview again, I had the nagging feeling we'd somehow missed our best opportunity for an exit.

TWENTY-NINE

WRECKS

THE GATES to Coconut Chuck's salvage yard stood open now. I pulled the Bronco through and had my first good look at the place from ground level. Boats made up the majority of the salvage inventory, with a few cars and a fair amount of planes rounding out the transportation casualties.

"Up around the corner on the right," Vaughn said from the back, directing me toward an army green DC-3 fuselage near the front fence that had been turned into a sort of trailer. A sign welded above the boarding door read OFFICE.

From ground level, the boneyard sprawled farther than I originally thought. Climbing vines had reclaimed many of the longest residents, and one car shell had a tree growing up through the rear window. If Tyson was here somewhere, I couldn't see him, but sight lines were short. It was almost as though someone had designed the place as a maze. Even the corrugated tin walls, left to weather to an aesthetic state of corrosion, still maintained a sturdy rigidity on closer viewing. They were also lined with a row of rusty barbed wire that I hadn't noticed before.

"Get out," Vaughn commanded from the back seat.

I climbed out of the Bronco and waited for Whitney to come around the front to join me.

It was noisy here, a percussion of clunks and thumps as the gusting wind slapped tree branches against abandoned car doors and busted boat hulls. Someone had even made a wind chime from car mufflers and tailpipes that punctuated the air with soulful tones like a tragic xylophone.

The DC-3 Fuselage had been leveled to a flight attitude, the tail brought up to meet a deck with wooden steps. The entrance door had been laminated with bamboo, and wouldn't have been out of place in the jungle of Vietnam. Vaughn instructed me to mount the steps and I did, trying the office door and finding it open.

I ducked to peer inside and found the modified interior was an amalgamation of original aircraft and some worse-for-wear office furniture. The far wall of the fuselage had been blown out to make room for a broad desk and some primer-spotted file cabinets. A private minibar sat behind the desk beneath a framed poster of the Blue Angels signed by the pilots. The rest of the office structure was uninsulated wood construction that housed two couches and a TV that still used a DVD player and a VHS player.

There was no sign of Chuck.

"Does he have a workshop somewhere?" I asked Vaughn. "Somewhere he'd keep plane parts?"

"Around back."

I descended the steps and headed that way, but paused when the path opened up and offered a view toward the water. The Cessna 182 sat near the water's edge, a ridge of salt already in evidence along the edge of the prop and more crystalizing on the hardware. I moved that way.

"Hey!" Vaughn shouted. "It's this way."

"I'm going to check out the engine on this thing real quick," I said. "See if any of the spark plugs are still usable. You want us out of here, don't you?"

Vaughn readjusted his pistol in the waistband of his jeans, but didn't stop me. "Be quick about it."

I gestured for Whitney to follow me and we made our way over to the wreck. It was a sad sight, the windshield bedecked with seaweed and grime. The left wing had been wrenched away from the fuselage by a few degrees, evidence of the hard impact.

"Are you going to be able to use something from this to fix your plane?" Whitney asked.

I kept my voice low. "No. It's not the same type of spark plugs. I just wanted an excuse for a closer look at it."

Vaughn had lingered behind, enough that Whitney and I had a modicum of privacy.

"This is the plane Fabienne crashed in?" Whitney asked.

"What's left of it." I squatted at the side of the engine and inspected what was visible beneath the bent top cowling. The bottom cowl was gone, along with several of the rubber mounts for it at the firewall.

The carburetor air box was gone, but the carburetor itself was still there, and all of the fuel system. The exhaust muffler shroud had an obvious chafe mark in the front—a hole worn through it, ostensibly from some part of the missing air box. The hole went all the way through to the muffler. It was a small hole, but enough that exhaust fumes could escape into the shroud and from there pass into the ducting for the cabin heat. A source of carbon monoxide that the Air Accident Investigation Division couldn't help but notice.

I studied the line of the orange SCAT hose that would have borne the toxic gases into the aircraft's cabin. My fingers found the air door at the firewall and felt the action of it. The rigging on it was loose. A maintenance issue, easily missed during an inspection, especially if viewed by an inexperienced mechanic.

After all, how often does the heater door even get opened in a tropical paradise?

An unfortunate, tragic accident.

But as my eyes roamed over the exhaust, I noted other things too. Shiny scuffed corners on the exhaust nuts. The slightly misaligned way the stacks sat against their gaskets. Like someone had put them on in a hurry. Almost certainly another cause for a leak. More apparent sloppy maintenance. It would certainly go in the report that way. Maybe some guy in the last place that worked on the plane would lose his license over it. AAID might insist on it.

But they'd be wrong.

"You going to salvage something?" Vaughn asked, behind me now, watching.

"Yeah. I just need a socket wrench and a spark plug socket. And a couple wrenches for these ignition wires. Can have it out in two minutes if I had those."

"Let's go then," he said and jerked his head toward the way we'd come. "Chuck's got tools in the shop."

We walked back down the narrow path between stacked carcasses of old cars, some dripping with flowering vines. We reached the maintenance shop. It was a block building with rolling bay doors. One door was up, the chain hanging loose and clinking in the wind. The garage had three bays, two were occupied by old cars, a slick custom Dodge Charger, and another old beater sedan. The back wall was lined with tool boxes and workbenches. Oil stains marked the floor. I walked around the one in the open bay and made my way to the nearest tool chest. Vaughn lingered in the doorway but pulled his gun loose from his pants. A room full of tools presented me with a lot of options and he wasn't oblivious to it.

"Just the wrenches," he said.

I pulled the top drawer of the tool chest open and scanned

the contents. A high quality Snap-On wrench set was front and center in the drawer. The nuts on the ignition leads took a 3/4 inch wrench, but I had something else in mind so I scooped up the longer one-inch wrench instead. The haft of it was nearly a foot long and it had a substantial weight in my hand. More than that, it felt familiar. I had an identical tool in my own box at home and knew the feel and weight of it from years of use.

I pulled the next drawer out, locating the socket set. The socket wrench had decent weight to it as well, and I attached the 1/2 inch drive spark plug socket to it and turned and walked back to the open door with it, my gait as casual as I could manage. A surge of adrenaline was pumping through me. The familiar jolt of anticipation. Fight or flight biology. I'd felt it enough in my life to recognize and enjoy it.

Vaughn must have sensed something too, because his posture changed at my approach. He glanced left to Whitney, but she was out of reach. He'd gotten sloppy, let her wander too far to make an effective shield. He might have raised the gun if he had the chance, but I tossed the socket wrench in a high arc above him, forcing him to look up.

"Catch."

It was a cheap move and I'm sure some part of him knew he should keep his eyes on me, but it's hard to ignore an airborne socket wrench when it's in a free fall toward your skull. To his credit, I think he might have caught the thing with his upraised hand had I not used the opportunity to bum rush him. My left hand caught his arm on its way up to block his face, and my right brought the wrench down hard, lacerating his brow above his right eye just as the socket wrench ricocheted off his shoulder. He slammed backward into the track for the rolling door, setting the chain jangling. He didn't go down so I swung again as he ducked, this time connecting with the back of his skull. He went down hard this time, crashing to the concrete floor face-first.

Whitney screamed, then quickly covered her mouth with her hands. "Oh my God."

When it became clear Vaughn wasn't getting back up, I lowered my wrench.

"Is he dead?" Whitney asked.

I honestly wasn't sure, so once I'd stepped on his pistol and slid it away from his grip, I crouched and put a couple of fingers to Vaughn's neck.

"He's still got a pulse."

"Holy shit," Whitney muttered. "You got him."

I picked up the Beretta M9 and checked the action on it. I ejected the magazine and verified the load. It was full.

"Let's find Tyson and get the hell out of—" A sudden prick in my abdomen caught me short. I looked down.

Just below my ribs, a dot of orange fluff had my shirt pinned to my abdominal muscles. I pinched the little tuft between my forefinger and thumb and it came free, pulling about an inch of silver dart with it. "What the hell?"

I looked up and Whitney's eyes were on a similar dart that now protruded from her shirt just above her left breast.

"Luke?"

I fell to my knees. Then my side. Whitney collapsed on top of me. Then the world went dark.

THIRTY
TIE DOWN

I CAME to under bright lights that made me squint. Felt like the worst hangover I'd had in years. I blinked a few times and tried to move. My arms were pinned down at my sides. My feet were immobile too. I was on my back, looking up at a low, unfinished industrial ceiling made of metal. An air duct was blowing cool air into the room, but otherwise the room was surprisingly quiet.

I rolled my head to the left and found Whitney lying in her own hospital bed a few feet away, feet and wrists likewise secured with Velcro straps. Her shirt had been removed, though she still wore a bra and her pencil skirt. There was an IV in her arm, the bag on a hook beside her. We were strapped to electric adjustable hospital beds, but this was no hospital.

A TV hung in the corner but the image was static, a security cam shot of the salvage yard's front gate. It shifted every few seconds to a different angle of The Boneyard. The walls of the room were OD green or eggshell white depending on which way you looked, and one of the green walls was decorated with framed photographs. Helicopters, jungles. Groups of soldiers in fatigues. One was a civilian group in a bar. And in each photo a younger, slimmer version of the man I knew as Coconut Chuck. I blinked twice and recognized one of the soldiers in the photos as Vaughn. He stood with his arm around Chuck's shoulders. Old friends.

Chuck.

I tilted my head up and looked at my abdomen. I was shirtless. The little pinprick of a spot where I'd been darted was still visible on my skin.

Tranquilizer dart.

I guess I knew who the unlucky seagull was now.

"Whit," I whispered, turning my head in the direction of the other bed. "Whitney! Can you hear me?"

A door opened and closed behind me.

"Don't think she'll be able to talk for a bit yet, hoss. Surprised you're awake." Coconut Chuck appeared around my right side and loomed over me. He had glasses on. Something I hadn't seen him in before. He wore another of his loud Hawaiian shirts and was breathing heavily through his nostrils. He had latex gloves on.

"What the hell are you doing?" I asked.

He peered down at me through the thick lenses. "What? You don't like my facility? Worked hard on this. Industrial ventilation, redundant water pumps." He waved an arm to encompass it all. "Two generators. We're ten feet underground. That storm that's revving up outside won't even make the lights blink. This is state of the art bunker-life, friend. We could ride out the apocalypse in here if we wanted to."

I laid my head back on the table. "Can't believe you darted us."

"You like that? Tough shot in the wind, too. If I didn't have the gusto, I might not have had the range." He patted his substantial belly. "Good thing I have it where it counts."

I stared up at the fluorescent overhead lights and cursed at myself for all the signs I'd missed.

"But I have to hand it to you, chief. You played a good game," Chuck said. "When I saw you sniffing around that 182 earlier, I knew you'd have to go. Something on it give me away? I thought I had that setup dialed in pretty good."

"There was no soot," I muttered toward the ceiling.

"How's that?"

I sighed. "The nuts are scuffed up. Shows someone wrenched that exhaust on recently. Couple of gaps in around the gaskets. The hole in the muffler shroud too. But if it had been running like that for any length of time, there would have been soot seeping out. There isn't any. You replaced the exhaust with a doctored one, something that looked like it caused an accidental CO leak, but you couldn't run it that way. And it shows."

"Ah. True enough. But not a worry. I'll just say the seawater washed it off."

"You ever try to get oily exhaust soot off your hands with just water?"

Chuck smiled. "You and I know that wouldn't work. But these AAID guys? Half of 'em don't know a tailpipe from a water bong. I'll be all right." He patted me on the shoulder. "Good thing I had a spare exhaust lying around, huh?"

"Off the wrong engine."

"Lucky I had anything at all that fit. Plane wasn't ever supposed to come back. What are the odds a good samaritan like you happens to be flying by in a seaplane of all things? I'd worried some about a boat seeing it go in, but I never planned for you."

"Glad I could put a wrench in the works."

"But there you go showing your lack of ignorance again. In this particular situation, exhaust off a four-seventy fits just fine on that O-520. Would it run great? Hell no. But I don't have to run shit, do I? That plane's reached its final destination. I'll buy the wreck off the insurance company for a song. Especially since I have a feeling that plane might take an additional beating in this weather. By the time AAID gets around to looking at it, if they ever do, I'll have all my ducks in a row and anyone who knows better will be long gone. Those chumps will buy any story I tell them, and probably nod along the whole time."

"You plan to dump us at sea? Feed us to your seagulls? What?"

"Plenty of options at my disposal, aren't there?" Chuck looked across me to the unconscious form of Whitney on the other table. "Trouble is, I'm not a man to let an opportunity go to waste. Here I've got myself two young healthy specimens like yourselves. Both of you keep yourselves in good shape. I can tell that much even without the blood tests. A guy who didn't know better would dump you overboard someplace and not know what he was missing. Old days when I was running with some of my boys from Chicago, we'd have tied some cinder blocks to your feet and said sayonara. But I'm sitting on four good kidneys here, two livers, two sets of lungs, even a couple healthy hearts. I'm sure most of that won't make it to a donor in time. With this storm restricting travel options, and ol' Doc Marcus swimming with the fishes, my options for resale are limited. But I've got some friends in Cuba desperate for my services.

"I won't get the kind of top dollar I usually do off the American crowd, but I'll still get ten grand a kidney at least in Havana. Maybe twenty." He counted off on his fingers. "Livers should get me fifty each. I'll have to find the right recipient. Shit's not as easy as it used to be and I'm getting a little out of practice."

"Lucrative business," I said. "And here we thought it was Dr. Marcus we had to worry about."

Chuck picked up a syringe. "You need a surgeon for the install, I'll give you that. You put me in an operating room trying to plug one of these things back in, your odds of getting a happy ending are low. But extraction's not bad. You've likely seen enough salvage operators parting out planes to know what I'm talking about. Don't need a mechanic's license to take shit apart. Planes and people are similar that way. Parts are parts in my book. Hold still now. I need to get a little more blood." He stuck me with the needle, taped it down, then connected the tubing connector like they used at blood banks. He filled a small vial of blood, checked it, then pulled a second for good measure.

"Black market organ deals still involve blood tests?"

"Surprisingly particular fuckers. You'd better believe it. But luckily there's a market for everything. People even take junkie's organs these days. Helps me out plenty when I can still get a set of lungs or a liver off some chump who OD'd on pills or snuff. You'd think it would disqualify them, but dying people have lower standards than the rest of us."

"Regular overdoses, or the kind Doc Marcus had?"

Chuck cocked his head at me and gave me that same look he had the first night I met him at the bar, and in that movement I saw the predator inside him for what it was. "Julian forgot which side he was on. Said he wanted out. So I let him out. Just not the out he wanted."

The seriousness of what I was in for settled into me. Chuck had killed at least two people I knew of in the last few days. A couple more wouldn't bother him.

He leaned in close, only inches from my face. "I'm not a man to put up with disloyalty. Julian knew the score. We'd been working together a long time and the contract we had was written in blood. He never served like you and me, but he should have understood. Spilling blood together bonds men for life. It's a pact."

"I bet that pact was costing him."

"A pittance." Chuck gestured toward the far wall with a hand still holding the vial of my blood. "He had a fortune coming in compliments of Solomon and her do-gooder fund. My cut was minimal. Just enough to keep the lights on, and to remind him who his first partner was."

He didn't bother to mention keeping the lights on aboard his state-of-the-art wrecker or submersible. I was guessing the blackmail from Marcus was more substantial than he was letting on, but now wasn't the time to start an argument. I did want to keep him talking though. Keep him from getting into worse parts of this process.

"That boat motor I heard last night. The two-stroke. That was your shore boat coming in from the salvage vessel." I said.

"Heard that, did you? You've got good ears." Chuck busied himself with something else on the medical cart. "Too bad there's no market for those."

"Being out in the wrecker makes a good alibi too. But if you were out at sea, how'd you know Marcus was leaving?"

"Little birdie told me," Chuck said. "Good thing I have a sat phone on the boat, huh?"

I flexed uselessly against the restraints.

"Where's Tyson?" I asked, not sure I wanted to know the answer.

Chuck set the rack of blood vials in a glass-fronted fridge on the neighboring countertop, then came back and leaned against the bed support with both hands. "That's a kick in the pants, ain't it? I can see how much you like that kid. I like him too. Would have been fun to train up a kid like that. Makes me remember how enthusiastic I was about everything at that age. Remember being that young? All we needed for a good time was a few buddies and some tail to chase."

He looked at the wall of photos. The younger him smiled back from the wall with his fellow soldiers. And the guys I assumed were his friends from Chicago.

"He's still alive?"

"Sent him back over to my hangar. Have him wrenching on an old T6 Texan cylinder I've got in the back there." He found the remote for the TV and cycled through views till he got to a camera that showed his hangar on the airfield. And Tyson was there, alive and rummaging around on a shelf of cylinder cores. "That boy's determined to do the job right and make you proud."

I swallowed hard and kept my eyes on the screen as Chuck did something with the zoom. "I'm already proud of him."

The zoom reached its limit, showing a grainy image of Tyson's face as he fitted a socket to the plug in the cylinder.

"Of course you know he can't live either," Chuck said.

My jaw clenched.

"Figure he'll have to go down with the Mallard when I scuttle it somewhere. I'll need to find a deep spot for it. Sad end for that old bird. I'll tell everyone I warned you not to fly in the storm." He pressed something on the remote and the screen went back to its view of the salvage yard. He tossed the remote to the counter and patted me on the shoulder. "But don't worry. I'm sure you'll both be missed." He moved to the door. "I'd better go get him soon. You'll have to excuse me. But we'll chat more, chief. Rest up. You're gonna have a tough day."

He went through the door and the lock clicked behind him.

I jerked at the restraints on my wrists and roared.

THIRTY-ONE
FLEX

THERE WAS no clock in the room. I'd lost my watch too, but I guessed it was about fifteen minutes later when Whitney spoke.

"Are you just going to lie there?"

I turned my head to find her blue eyes staring at me.

"Good to see you're awake."

"Thought I was dreaming there for a bit, but I think I was just in a haze. That fat guy was here, talking."

"You heard that?"

"Hmm. Some of it. Sounds like he's going to kill us."

"Looks that way." I resumed my stare at the ceiling.

"You need to get us out of here then."

"Why didn't I think of that?" I muttered and jerked at my bonds again.

I turned and found her still staring at me, her eyes glossy, like the haze of the tranquilizer drugs was still affecting her some. "So you're giving up? You're gonna let us die?"

I clenched my jaw again and bit back my rage. My debilitating helplessness. My mouth tasted like failure.

"You're the captain," she muttered. "You're in charge of transportation."

"Our flight seems to have been permanently delayed. Mechanical issues." I jerked futilely at the wrist restraints again.

"You're doing it . . . wrong," she said. She studied me, then squirmed on her bed. "You need to use . . . your hips."

I watched as she rotated her knee and torso, then used an admirable amount of core strength to slowly pull herself vertical. In the end, her wrists and ankles were still bound and she was hunched over, but she was sitting upright. "See?"

I did see.

She pulled at her straps, but gave up after a brief effort. "Not that I'm sure what we do from here."

I mimicked the motions she had used, but my first effort left me gasping back on the bed.

"Come on," she said. "I know you're more flexible than that. Imagine me naked if you have to. Is that your only motivator?"

I gritted my teeth again and made another attempt. The muscles of my abdomen and arms strained as I fought my way up from an elbow, but this time I pushed through the pain and made it upright.

"Hot damn," I muttered.

"He didn't use a chest restraint on us," she said. "Maybe he forgot what abs were."

"Too busy working on his blow dart skills," I said, fighting to loosen my arm restraints again. The Velcro straps around my wrists were still tight, but I had significantly more leverage sitting up. Putting some back into it, I curled hard against whatever the strap was attached to.

"Come on, tell me a man is good for something," Whitney goaded.

I groaned through my clenched teeth and pulled for all I was worth—and something finally gave way. It wasn't much, but something moved.

"What was that?" Whitney asked.

"Probably my future hernia," I said. But I took a deep breath and pulled again. This time the restraints on both sides moved slightly. I began rocking back and forth, alternating pressure against whatever it was I was pulling on.

"It's bending the rail," Whitney said, watching from her bed. "You're moving it."

I continued to cold work the metal rails the straps were connected to, back and forth, back and forth. It was only a fraction of an inch at a time, but I kept at it. I tried to imagine the molecules of metal getting as angry as I was, heating up and flexing against each other. "Come on," I muttered, practically thrashing at this point. Beads of sweat dripped down my chest. My arms were on fire, but I didn't let up. Everything had a breaking point. I was going to push the limits of mine.

"It's flexing farther. Keep going!" Whitney said.

And with one last Herculean pull, something gave way. My right arm came loose. The strap dangling from my wrist was now disconnected from the lower bed rail it had been attached to.

"Hell, yeah." I wasted no time freeing the Velcro on my other wrist, followed by the first wrist and my ankles. I leapt out of the bed and freed Whitney.

I'd just yanked the needle and tube fitting out of my arm when she slid off of the bed and wrapped her arms around me.

She didn't say a word, but she squeezed hard.

"Me too," I said. "Let's get the hell out of here."

She went straight for the door but the handle didn't move.

I was already looking for different options.

"What do we do?" Whitney asked. "No windows."

"Luckily, this room wasn't designed to keep people in," I said, rummaging through drawers. "It's a bunker. Meant to keep people out. That's why the door hinges are on our side."

Whitney studied the door and the two silver hinges that protruded inward.

"We just need a way to get the pins free." I found a drawer with odds and ends that included a small screwdriver. "And something to use as a hammer," I said. That was going to be more difficult. But I moved to the bed and checked for anything useful on it. Whitney opened a cabinet and found our clothes and some of our other belongings sitting on a shelf. There was also a portable oxygen cylinder in there. "Hand me that," I said. She passed over the cylinder. It was solid. Not the wisest choice to use something under pressure as a hammer, but I opened the valve on it and started letting the oxygen out so if I did accidentally puncture it while using it, maybe it wouldn't be as catastrophic.

I moved to the hinges and got to work. Whitney shrugged back into her top, then picked up my Swiss Army knife and wallet from the pile. "This yours?"

"I'll take it."

"No phones," she said. "Vaughn must still have them."

"Might still be in the Bronco if we can get to it."

I'd worked the lower hinge pin loose enough to get it free so I used that to get the next one moving.

"He's going to hear all that racket," Whitney said.

I gestured toward the TV with my head. "See if you can find him."

She picked up the remote and figured out how to move the view. The camera angles were all exterior of the salvage yard or the airplane hangar. Nothing inside the bunker.

"Wait, is that him?"

She'd stopped on a view of the front gate and it showed a pair of headlight beams entering the yard. The SUV looked familiar.

"Shit," I muttered. "That's Swain."

"That's good though, right? He can help us."

"But we need to warn him about Chuck."

"Maybe you'd better hurry," Whitney said. As we watched, Chuck walked into the frame.

I knocked the top hinge pin the rest of the way loose and it clattered to the floor.

The door came free from the jam and I let it fall inward, where it landed partly atop one of the hospital beds.

Whitney tossed me my shirt and I slipped my arms into it as I moved out into the hallway of the bunker. There were several other rooms. I peeked into a couple quickly.

"I think the stairs are this way," Whitney said.

"Hang on one second. I'm trying to improve our odds."

"How?"

"You ever known a man to build an apocalypse bunker and not also keep firearms?"

"The two do seem to go together," she said.

"Let's hope." I rifled through the few rooms of the bunker in a hurry. There was a full gun safe against one wall that was locked, but I was hoping a guy like Chuck kept an ace in the hole somewhere. I struck out in the bunk room, but feeling around beneath the desk in the room with the stairs that served as an office, my fingers hit metal. I pulled the pistol loose and it turned out to be an antique M1911. I popped the magazine out and it carried a full load of seven, plus one already in the chamber. Ready to rock and roll.

Would have loved to see a spare mag lying around but I wasn't that lucky. Still, our circumstances were vastly improved. "Let's get going," I said, and led the way to the stairs and climbed up to ground level.

That's where our luck ran out. The metal bunker door was locked. And the hinges had sealed industrial strength pins. There was a sliding window in the door. I moved the slide and was able to peer out into the salvage yard but the door wouldn't budge. There might have been a padlock on the outside. Whatever it was, the door wasn't opening.

"Shit," I muttered. "I can't see Swain." The view out the sliding window was obscured by a pile of cars. Wind buffeted the surrounding bushes and shrubs.

"What now?" Whitney asked.

"Back down, look for another exit. An emergency hatch or something."

We scrambled back down the stairs and searched the rooms again, this time checking the ceilings and any other place an exit might be hidden.

But our search was cut short by a rattling of the lock at the top of the stairs.

"Someone's coming," Whitney said. "We've got to hide."

But I took one look around the rooms we'd ransacked for a gun and knew there was no hiding. The door from Chuck's operating room certainly wasn't going back on. So I pushed Whitney behind me and we backed down the hall. When Chuck's pudgy gut came down those steps, I was going to blast it full of holes.

I lifted the pistol, aimed for the top of the stairs, and waited as the footsteps sounded on the landing. The steps were steady and unhurried. But when the shoes and legs came into view, the thin trousers were navy with red stripes down the sides and the man who descended into view wasn't Chuck. It was Edwin Swain.

He took a look around the disheveled room and his eyes finally landed on me and the gun.

We locked eyes.

"Mr. Angel. I wondered when you'd get to the bottom of this."

THIRTY-TWO

SWAIN

EDWIN SWAIN WORE a Glock 17 in a hip holster. My primary focus at the moment was that it stayed there.

"You can put the weapon down, Luke," Swain said.

It was the first time I'd heard him use my first name. He appeared calm, unaffected by my disheveled appearance and the pistol I had aimed at him.

"I'd like you to keep your hands where I can see them," I said.

"I'm the police, Luke. You can relax. Miss Gilton, I see you're caught up in this too. Don't worry. We'll straighten things out."

"Where's Chuck?" I asked, eyeing the stairs beyond him.

"Said he was headed for the airfield. Helping someone out over there. I just came down to use his landline. Storm's taken out cell service on the island."

"I'd like you to turn around and put your hands up against the wall."

Swain shook his head slowly. "That's not how things work around here, Luke. I'm the constable. I'm the law."

"When it's convenient?"

"You've found yourself in a scary situation here," Swain said. "It's okay to be upset. Just put the gun down and let's talk."

"After you turn around and put your hands against the wall."

Swain's eyes flashed this time. A muscle twitched in his jaw. "You're out of line, son. Time to stand down."

"We're going to walk up those stairs in sixty seconds," I said. "I'd prefer to do it without hurting anyone, but after the day we've had, I'm becoming less particular about that."

"You're not going to shoot a police officer. I don't think that's what you want." He took a couple of steps toward me.

"You might be surprised."

He spread his hands. "We're on the same team, Luke. It's Vaughn and his boys you're after. Running drugs, poisoning this island. I'm not the one you have an issue with."

"Would Ruth Solomon agree with you?" Whitney asked from beside me. She came around to face Swain. "We talked to Mama Jacqui. We know everything."

"Jacqui?" Swain scoffed. "What does she know? Did Marcus talk to her?" His brow furrowed and his mocking expression shifted to concern. "What did he tell her?"

Whitney pressed him. "We know his drug problem was tied to Ruth Solomon. It was all her fault, wasn't it?"

"You leave Ruth out of this." Swain raised a finger and pointed at Whitney. "The last thing I'll tolerate is some outsider coming in and disparaging one of the finest women on this island."

"Thirty seconds," I said.

But the fury rose in Swain's voice. "It's the goddamn press like you that we've had to clear out for years. Always after a story. Digging and digging. Trying to throw dirt on Mali and her mother and turn this quiet little island into something it isn't. For you, we're just a piece of tinder you can burn up in your furnace of twenty-four hour news stories. You don't care who it hurts or what it costs us. Just so long as you get your byline on the homepage of a website for a few hours."

"You've got an illegal organ smuggler in a bunker on your quiet little island," I said. "A bunker you somehow have a key to."

He glared at me.

"Ten seconds," I added.

His lip curled and he looked from me to Whitney and back. "That's the problem with this younger generation. No understanding of higher purpose. Of sacrifice for something greater than yourselves. A small island protects its own. Whatever the cost." His right hand came up with the Glock in it, faster than I'd anticipated.

But I squeezed the trigger three times and put three rounds from the .45 directly into his chest. The older man staggered back against the wall, hit it hard, then slumped down it to a sitting position. By the time his chin hit his chest, he was dead.

Whitney had put her hands over her ears reflexively from the noise. My ears rang too from the report of the gun echoing in such a confined space, but I kept the barrel aimed at Swain's skull till I was able to get closer and kick the Glock loose from his fingertips. I dragged it toward me with the toe of my shoe.

When I was satisfied Swain was no longer a threat, I stooped and picked up the Glock to inspect it. I turned to Whitney. "You know how to use a firearm?"

"As much as I appreciate that you think I might," she held up her hands, "that's going to be your department."

"You goaded him into talking. You got in his head."

"Yeah, well. That's my gift. You're welcome."

"You knew he was in on this?"

"Honestly, I was as surprised as you."

"Damn. You're good then. All that stuff you threw out about Ruth Solomon. You really struck a nerve."

"What can I say? I'm good at my job. Some of it means fishing for clues the hard way."

I tucked the M1911 into the back of my pants and checked the mag on the Glock. "Bet no one ever called you the Benoit Blanc of Florida, though."

"Would I ever want them to?"

I shrugged. "Yeah, I see your point. Come on. Let's get out of here."

THIRTY-THREE

CHARGER

THE RAIN WAS COMING down slantways when we made it outdoors.

Darkness had overtaken the island, compliments of the storm that now stretched from one horizon to the other.

Droplets of rain pummeled rusty cars and old boat hulls, adding a steady new rhythm to the already windy cacophony of the salvage yard.

I squinted into the murk, trying to orient our heading in a sky devoid of sun.

"This way," I said and pointed a direction I hoped was toward the front gate.

Whitney shielded her eyes from the rain and stayed on my heels.

Chuck's bunker sat deep in the maze of his salvage yard, but after a couple of wrong turns, I spotted the garage we'd been in with Vaughn. From there it was a straight shot to the Bronco at the front gate. Except, it wasn't the only vehicle in sight. The SUV belonging to Constable Swain was still there, and so was Vaughn's truck. The sight brought me up short.

He'd ridden with us to get here, meaning sometime since we'd been confined in Chuck's bunker, he'd recovered from his blow to the head enough to leave, and he'd come back. That, or someone had come in his truck to pick him up. I wasn't sure which scenario I liked worse. Either way, he was still here.

A bullet ricocheted off a truck hood beside me and answered the question for me. More gunfire erupted from our left and I thrust Whitney to the ground behind a fenderless Volkswagen Beetle body.

"Stay down," I shouted and poked my head up only enough to catch the muzzle flash from my eleven o'clock. A security guard I vaguely recognized from the Solomon party was walking brazenly forward, firing off steady shots that perforated the Beetle's front trunk and fractured the glass into spiderwebs of shards. He'd have us in clear view in a matter of five steps, but his posture made me think he didn't know I was armed. I waited only a second to get my feet firmly under me, then popped up and fired three quick shots from the Glock. The first flew wide in the wind, but the second and third hit the guy high in the thigh and through his left arm respectively. He yelped as he fell and he rolled in the mud briefly before scrambling on all fours back toward an adjacent scrap pile, his pistol forgotten in the mud. I could have put another round up his tailpipe from my angle, but more gunfire from beyond him made me duck for cover.

"There are at least two more," I said to Whitney. "And they'll flank us quick if they have any sense. We've got to move." I pointed toward the open bay of the garage. "When I say, you run."

She nodded wordlessly and got to her feet.

"Go!"

I popped up again and unloaded a barrage of bullets in the direction I'd seen the muzzle flashes.

Whitney didn't hesitate, but shot off from a sprinter's stance and practically flew. She cleared the distance to the garage so fast I don't think our attackers had time to react. She'd made it look so easy that I took off after her, firing one-handed toward the vehicle I'd spotted Vaughn behind. They fired back this time however, and just before I hit the safety of the garage, a searing hot pain ripped across my back. I missed a step but kept my feet, then careened into the corner of the open garage bay, colliding with a rolling workbench and sending tools skittering across the floor. Whitney wasted no time slamming her hand into the electric door button and the bay door began its descent. Two more bullets struck the wall outside, chipping cinderblock and sending dust up, but no one immediately pursued us inside. The rolling door clanked to the floor with a welcome finality.

We'd bought ourselves a moment of safety, but it was precarious. I peeked out the garage's one shoulder-high barred window above the workbench and tried to glimpse movement, but the rain and murk made it too difficult, so I ducked clear again.

"You're hurt," Whitney said.

"Wasn't born with your speed. You train with Gail Devers or something?" I felt my back and my fingertips came away bloody. But I could already tell it wasn't fatal. "I think it just grazed my ribs. I've had worse."

Whitney looked skeptical but had her own concerns. "Will they come in after us?"

I imagined she already knew the answer. The garage that had formerly offered salvation now seemed claustrophobic. We were foxes in a hole. I spotted a back door with a chain on it, but it was going to be the first route Vaughn would expect us to flee. As I scanned the garage in search of any other options, my eyes landed on the Dodge Charger on the lift.

Maybe it was too many *Dukes of Hazzard* reruns as a kid, but the Charger gave me an idea. This fox still had a few moves left.

I walked to the car and looked under it. Engine was in. Wheels and brakes all looked intact. I hit the lift button and lowered the car.

"You've got to be kidding," Whitney said.

"We're not getting to the Bronco. We need another ride. So guess who gets to open the garage door."

The car settled to the floor.

"You're a son of a bitch," Whitney muttered. "First thing I'm doing when I get home is learning to drive a stick."

"If you knew that, you never would've met me," I said and moved around the car to the driver's side. The keys were in the cup holder.

A bullet shattered the glass in the window above the workbench and we both flinched and ducked.

"Sounds pretty good right now!" Whitney shouted, but she went to the door button on the wall. I climbed into the Charger and inserted the keys in the ignition. I winced once when the wound on my back hit the seat cushion, but then leaned across and flung the passenger door open.

"As soon as this thing starts, mash that and jump in."

I stuck the Glock in the cupholder, then pulled the M1911 from my waistband and laid it on the passenger seat. Then I put the Charger in reverse, depressed the clutch and cranked the engine. The V8 came to life with a single pump of the accelerator, belching out a plume of exhaust that made Whitney cough. The sound was accompanied by muffled shouting from outside.

More glass shattered from the window on the far wall of the garage, but this time it was someone smashing out the panes with the butt of a pistol and reaching in to fire. I picked up the M1911 from the passenger seat and fired two shots in that direction, one of which struck the pistol protruding through the window. The arm with the gun vanished again with a volley of swearing.

Whitney mashed the garage door button and lunged for the car, plunging inside and ducking while she reached for the door handle. My view out the back windshield showed the rising door followed by the hips and torso of someone blocking the path with a gun.

He'd picked a poor place to stand.

The rear wheels of the Charger squealed when I let out the clutch and the car rocketed backward faster than the guy could dodge. I clipped him with the bumper and sent him up and over the trunk lid. Whitney barely had her door closed in time to avoid hitting him with that too. I spotted Vaughn at the far side of the garage under the eaves and he raised his pistol. "Head down!" I shouted to Whitney, but she was already ducking low.

There wasn't a lot of road to maneuver the Charger, but I got enough speed to flick the wheel hard and torque the car into a Rockford turn, shifting to second gear as the front end spun around and letting out the clutch again once we were headed forward. A bullet ripped through the rear windshield, spiderwebbing the glass just before I made it past a stack of cars. But it was just as well. There was no looking back now. I wrenched the wheel around to the left again, circling the junk pile and rocketing back toward the gate.

Vaughn was out in the open still firing at us as we came into view again, but I was ready too. I upshifted to third, grabbed the Glock with my left hand and hung it out the window, unloading the rest of the magazine in Vaughn's direction as we flew toward the gate. The engine roared as the RPMs redlined in third, but we blasted out the gate past Vaughn's truck and into the darkness beyond.

I dropped the empty Glock to the floorboards and took a better grip on the wheel to shift gears again. Whitney finally lifted her head from the cringing crash position she'd curled into in the passenger seat and tried to look out the rear windshield. I checked the side view mirror.

If Vaughn was still back there, I couldn't see him. And he wouldn't catch the Charger in his pickup. I had no intention of sticking around to see his next move.

Whitney pressed herself into the full depth of the bucket seat and gripped the door handle. "Good God that was scary. I swear I'm never asking for another assignment in the field."

"We're getting out of here, right now."

The windsock at the corner of the airfield was standing straight out.

"Can you fly in this?" Whitney asked.

"We're sure as hell going somewhere. As soon as I find my copilot."

The tires chirped as I made the turn to the airfield, but I didn't slow down for the fence in the parking lot.

"Oh Jesus," Whitney exclaimed as I put the Charger straight through the section of chain link beside the gate. The fencing broke loose from the post and sprung up and away from the car as I careened through. I torqued the wheel around hard once more on the tarmac to get to the front of the lone hangar on the field. I locked up the wheels and skidded to a stop just outside the pedestrian door for the hangar.

Whitney finally released her death grip on the door handle and exhaled. "I sure hope you fly better than you drive."

Tropic Angel beckoned from the ramp, a dim silhouette outlined in mist from the pummeling rain.

But the lights were still on inside the hangar.

"Get to the plane," I said. "I'll be right behind you."

Without waiting for a response, I climbed out of the Charger and strode through the slanting rain with the M1911 in my grip. The pulsing of blood in my ears was a war drum spurring me on.

The door was unlocked and I flung it wide, letting it slam against the side of the hangar in the wind.

I was through the door in a moment, gun up.

"Tyson!" I shouted.

The overhead lights flickered, buzzing from a sudden surge. Then Chuck's voice rang out from the far side of the Piper Navajo. "Right this way, chief!" His voice echoed from the hangar walls then was lost amid the thrumming of rain on the metal roof.

Mali Solomon's Embraer sat in the corner of the hangar to my left.

I aimed the pistol in the direction I'd heard Chuck's voice, circling wide around the Navajo's empennage, sweeping the barrel across every hint of a threat beyond.

But when I got around the tail of the Navajo, Chuck came into clear view. He was looking right at me, a cool smile on his lips. He held a Beretta pistol in one meaty hand, but it wasn't aimed at me. His other arm was clamped around Tyson's neck and the muzzle of the pistol was pressed to the boy's head.

THIRTY-FOUR
STANDOFF

I HAD three bullets left in the M1911 but none of them were doing me a bit of good.

"I love situations like this, don't you?" Chuck said. "They show you what a man's made of."

I still had my gun up but Chuck was careful to speak from behind Tyson. He outweighed the boy by a hundred pounds and wasn't having much trouble keeping him pinned. Tyson's cheeks were wet, but his jaw was set now, holding back emotions as best he could.

"It's all right, Ty," I said. "Hang in there."

"He said he's gonna kill me if I don't tell him what I know. Told him I don't know anything."

"That's not all the way true, is it?" Chuck crooned in his ear. "You told me plenty. Told me about the Haitian girl waiting out in the plane. Gotta visit her next, don't I?"

Tyson grit his teeth. "I hope all your ketchup gets watery, you bus-driver-assed poser."

Chuck laughed. "You hear that, Angel? He hopes my ketchup gets watery."

"Personally, I'd like to say a lot worse."

"I think the worst is going to be on your end, chief," he said. "'Less you got the balls to end this now. What do you think? Gonna shoot me through the kid, sacrifice him to get to me? What's your play?"

"How about you let him go and we discuss it alone."

"You know I won't. And you know I got what it takes to vent his brains at you and sleep like a baby after. How about you? Enough ice in your veins to watch him die, or you gonna put that piece down and kick it over here?"

"You'll kill us both if I do."

"I'll kill you quick though, this time. Considering you MacGyvered your way out of those restraints so easily. Clock's ticking though. My trigger finger's getting itchy."

He pulled Tyson's face up against his so tightly their cheeks touched.

The relentless rain continued its assault on the hangar roof, thrumming in my head. Lightning flashed outside and shadows danced across the floor. I focused on Tyson.

"Just shoot this clown," Tyson said. "He's got it coming."

I sighted along the barrel of the M1911, but there was no good shot. Not with Chuck swaying with Tyson in his grip. He kept the pistol in the way too, and his laughing grin taunted me from behind it. Tyson's eyes locked on mine. "Just do it." His voice had a new edge.

"You a man of your word, Chuck? Soldier to soldier?"

"When it suits me."

"I'm going to put this gun down and kick it over. Only thing I ask is that you trade me for him in the lineup. You need to shoot somebody, you shoot me first. Clean. Then I don't have to see anything else."

"No!" Tyson shouted. But Chuck jerked his neck upward, choking off the cry.

"You trying to play hero?" Chuck asked, alert for a trick. "You got a second gun?"

"One gun. Yours. And I'm going to give it back. All you have to do is promise to shoot me first. I've seen enough people die in my life. I don't want to be around to watch this one."

"Your call, compadre. But let me see you do it."

I kept my eyes on Tyson as I slowly canted the pistol to one side and ejected the magazine from the M1911. Then I racked the slide and ejected the round from the chamber.

Tyson's eyes widened as I crouched low enough to drop the weapon to the floor.

"Well, I'll be damned," Chuck said. "You're dumber than you look."

But he took the barrel of his own pistol away from Tyson's temple and pointed it at me.

"No!" Tyson shouted again, but this time he did it with a big backswing of his elbow that caught Chuck in the ribs so hard it bent him over. Chuck swore and shoved Tyson away.

I lunged forward to charge him and gunfire erupted. I thought I was too late, somehow taking bullets, but it wasn't Chuck's Beretta doing the shooting. Something hit him in the shoulder and made him spin left.

"Die, you goddamn son of a bitch!" Fabienne shouted, appearing from around the front of the Navajo with her target pistol o.22 flashing. The little pops from the weapon were accompanied by pings and tings as the bullets ricocheted off the parts racks behind Chuck. Chuck swore and fired back wildly. In the chaos I grabbed Tyson by the arm and hauled him with me under the tail of the Navajo and sprinted toward the still open pedestrian door.

"Fabienne!" Tyson shouted as we ran.

I looked behind us and saw Chuck vanish between the parts racks clutching his head. Fabienne continued firing, the one good thing about the smaller caliber ammunition being that her little Sig Sauer pistol held a lot of it.

But every magazine runs out eventually, and faster than you'd like.

"Run!" I shouted, praying she heard me over the din of the rain and the pops from her weapon.

She must have realized the dangers of firing at a person who has better cover, because she turned and ran, firing two last shots into the parts shelves for good measure.

I nearly collided with Whitney on the way out the side door. She looked half-drowned from the rain but had evidently been lingering just outside as Fabienne snuck in.

"Is she okay?" she shouted to me, as I grabbed her by the shoulders and shoved her toward the plane.

"She's coming!"

And a moment later I was proven correct when Fabienne leapt through the door behind us, turning and sprinting after us. All four of us ran headlong through the wind and rain, all eyes on the seaplane waiting on the ramp.

"Luke, hold up!" Tyson shouted, grabbing my arm. "That spark plug, I left it in there! I dropped one when I took it out and was trying to replace it."

"We've got bigger problems," I shouted and pulled him onward.

"That cylinder's going to be dead."

"Good thing it's got nine!" I shouted back. "Is everything else together?"

"Mostly," Tyson yelled. "But that left engine's gonna run like shit."

"I've got another plug, but we don't have time to waste putting it in. Let's hope the other eight cylinders do their job."

"You had a spare plug this whole time? And you couldn't text me that?"

"I was a little tied up!"

I pointed him toward the engine. "Make sure it's buttoned enough to fly and pull all the chocks and gust locks. I'll crank the other engine first." I dashed around the plane, doing one quick check and yanking the nearest aileron gust locks loose, then ran for the boarding ladder and helped Whitney get her foot up the ladder.

"Luke, look!" She pointed toward the hangar, and I turned to see light spilling from beneath the huge hangar door. It was opening slowly, folding upward and evoking a groan like the hinges of a coffin lid. Except the person on the other side we only wished was dead.

"Go! Go!" Fabienne shouted. She still had her pistol, and she aimed it toward the hangar, but it was a slim comfort with the wind and at this range. I scrambled up the ladder behind Whitney and moved along the aisle at the center of *Tropic Angel* till I reached the flight deck. When I slid into the pilot seat, I risked a look out the pilot window toward the hangar again. By now the door was halfway up and I had a clear view of Chuck standing at the door controls, part of his face darkened by a smear of blood coming down from his hairline. He stood staring out at us, hand steady on the door switch, like he had all the time in the world.

"What's he doing?" Whitney asked, perched in the entryway of the flight deck looking past me toward the hangar.

I didn't know, but I also wasn't sure I wanted to find out.

Chuck lifted his pistol and fired off a shot toward us, missing somewhere, but a second shot made a plink in the rear cabin.

My fingers flew over the controls, priming the right engine, flipping on fuel pumps and lights. I cranked the window open.

"Clear right!" I shouted into the darkness.

I hit the starter and the right engine cranked over, taking only a few turns of the prop to fire. It rumbled to life, sending a spray of water against the hull and setting the whole plane vibrating.

"What the hell is that?" Fabienne shouted from the cabin, as another bullet found the plane.

Tyson was still outside. I revved the right engine and used the thrust to spin the aircraft around its left wheel, hoping to give Tyson some cover as he ducked behind the wing.

Tyson finished his run around the plane for the gust locks and shouted something to me through the wind that I couldn't make out. I simply waved him aft and prepped the left engine for start. He tossed the stepladder and gust locks to the ground and disappeared from view.

A bullet struck the windshield and imbedded itself in the plexiglass.

"Stop shooting my plane!" I turned to Whitney. "Tell me when he's in."

She looked aft toward the tail. "Not yet."

The left engine coughed and wheezed but didn't start. I tried again. This time it caught and fired but the rumble was uneven, the dead cylinder setting up a distinctly different vibration from the other engine.

"Will it fly like that?" Whitney asked.

"We're about to find out." I glanced out the right window again, dreading what I'd see. Chuck had the entire hangar door up now and he walked calmly around the tail of the big twin-engine Navajo. I could only make out his feet, but then they vanished. He was climbing aboard.

"Shit," I muttered and started rolling.

"Tyson's still not in yet!" Whitney shouted over the din.

"Tell him to hurry up. We gotta go!"

Whitney vanished back down the aisle in search of Tyson and I added some thrust to the engine. I looked back toward the tail and finally saw Tyson making his way forward.

"You trying to run me over or something?"

"You trying to get left behind?"

He slid into the copilot seat as I throttled up on the engines, using differential thrust to aid in the turn toward the taxiway.

"Dude, why's your back so bloody?"

"I got grazed by a bullet."

"Oh shit, Fabienne shot you?"

"I'll fill you in later. Strap in. This is about to get hairy." I pulled onto the taxiway and raced toward the departure end of the runway. The gusting crosswind had me fighting to keep the plane straight.

Tyson reached for the harness. "Real talk though, back there in the hangar—did you know Fabienne was there with the gun the whole time when you put yours down?"

"No."

"No? What the hell did you do that for then? You coulda got us both killed."

"I knew if I gave you the right motivation, you'd man up."

"Me? Against Chuck?"

"It worked. You hit him, didn't you?"

"Holy shit. Yeah, I guess I did."

"You told me the next time I needed you, you'd have my back. You kept your promise."

Tyson grinned wide. "Damn. I guess we're even then."

"Better hold off on the celebration. We're not out of this yet."

"Because of the bad engine?"

"Because of him," I said and pointed out the windshield as I made the turn onto the runway.

In the time it had taken us to taxi to the end of the runway, Chuck had started the Navajo and taxiied it out too. But instead of trying to pursue us, he'd taken the opposite taxiway and was now pulling the big twin onto the opposing end of the runway.

Fabienne appeared in between our seats and stared out into

the dark ahead, just as Chuck turned onto the runway and flicked on his wingtip-mounted landing lights. The beams refracted off the falling rain and illuminated the gloom.

"What the hell is that?" Fabienne asked.

"An obstacle," I said, gritting my teeth.

"Holy shit," she muttered.

"He wants to play chicken? Then we're gonna play chicken." I reached up for the throttles and pressed them full forward. On the far end of the runway, Chuck did the same.

THIRTY-FIVE
AIR TO AIR

RAIN LASHED the window of the Mallard as the engines hit full power. We were light on fuel and rolled forward fast despite the loud pops and grumbles from the left engine as it misfired on its lowest cylinder. *Tropic Angel* surged down Runway 9, building speed. The airspeed indicator came alive early in the gusting quartering headwind.

On the opposite side of the runway, the Piper Navajo threw up a halo of water in its prop wash as it throttled up to meet us.

"This guy's suicidal," Tyson shouted. "We're gonna crash."

"Just hold on!" I kept my hand on the throttles as *Tropic Angel* hurtled down the runaway, with me fighting the wind to keep it centered.

The Mallard weighed over twelve thousand pounds. The Navajo Chieftain was lighter, maybe six grand depending on load and fuel, but it would make no difference if we collided. Airplanes weren't built to make contact with anything but air and runways, so every foot of asphalt that vanished between our two aircraft only ensured our mutual destruction.

Tyson had a white-knuckled grip on his armrests in the

copilot's seat and he looked ready to flee aft toward the exit at any moment. "This plan is super sus, dude!" he shouted, nearly crawling backward up his seat.

Out the window, the Navajo roared toward us, eating up runway and closing the gap at an alarming rate.

The collision was imminent. Even if I slammed on the brakes now, there was no chance we'd stop in time, especially with Chuck coming on like a bat out of Hell. But I had no intention of stopping. Instead, just when it seemed certain we'd meet in a fiery inferno in the middle of the runway, I yanked the throttle for the left engine to idle, kept the right throttle firewalled, and mashed the left brake and rudder pedal, sending *Tropic Angel* into a hard left turn, off the runway, just clearing Chuck's hell-for-leather assault and careening over the apron grass toward the berm dividing the airfield from the neighboring cove. We hit the berm at full speed and got airborne. I came out of my seat as everything in the plane went weightless.

I slammed the left engine throttle full forward in midair, doing what I could to gain thrust and help the big bird stay airborne, but we didn't have enough airspeed. The Mallard flew fifty yards, just clearing the dock, then hit the surface of the cove with a gigantic splash, plowing bow-first into the waves and sending a geyser of seawater skyward. Tyson and I both slammed into the yokes and I heard shouts of alarm from the cabin.

The wave from our bow thundered onto the top of the plane and washed over the windscreen. The engines sputtered and choked, props flinging water all directions as the flying boat surged upward again and found her buoyancy in the darkening cove.

"Holy shit!" Tyson shouted from beside me.

I did a quick assessment of the plane's gauges. The engines had somehow stayed running, and despite the dramatic impact with the water, we were still afloat. Whether we stayed that way was another thing altogether.

"Get the landing gear up!" I shouted to Tyson. "We've got to move."

The wind across the cove was cutting tops off waves and already pushing us back toward shore. If we wanted any chance to not run aground back against the seawall, we needed to reduce drag in the water and give ourselves a fighting chance. I readjusted the throttles while Tyson hit the landing gear controls.

We both waited a tense few seconds, praying to God that the impact with the water hadn't damaged the amphibious landing gear. But the green lights blinked out, and a few moments later, I felt the reassuring thud as the hydraulics stowed the main wheels back against the hull.

Out the front windshield, the sea and sky roiled in displeasure, but we were still in action. I throttled up again, attempting to time our impacts with the oncoming waves.

"This is going to be rough," I said. "Hold onto your ass."

Tyson finally got belted into his harness. "Something worse than what you've done already?"

A call came from the cabin. "Luke?"

"What?"

"Is there supposed to be water back here?"

I craned my neck to see back down the aisle of the cabin and noted the glistening on the floor Whitney was pointing to. That and the tiny hole in the right side of the fuselage from one of Chuck's bullets that had found its way south of the waterline.

"You've got to be kidding me," I muttered. Then I shouted aft, "Stick a rag in it!"

"What rag?"

"Anything!"

If we got moving fast enough, the holes wouldn't matter

much, but the longer we stayed in the water, the tougher we'd have it. There might be more holes elsewhere.

We'd weathervaned to port in the current and I glanced left out the window and tried to get a look at the airfield.

Chuck's Navajo had stayed on the runway, but slowed to a taxi speed at the far end. Now it was turning around.

"Thank God that bastard can't float, huh?" Tyson said, watching the action as well.

But I didn't share his sense of relief, because as I made the turn toward the outlet of the cove, the Navajo on the runway throttled up again for takeoff into the wind.

"Oh hell no," Tyson said. "He's not still trying to get us out here, is he?"

"Shit, shit, shit," I swore, and focused all my attention on the churning water ahead.

The swells continued to slam into us, but the airspeed indicator needle showed signs of life. As I steered the aircraft with laboring thrust through the troughs, I slowly found our head in the wind and the plane gained speed knot by painful knot. Each impact with the oncoming waves sent shudders through our hull and caused me to grit my teeth. One particularly large swell came up over the bow and threatened to send us under for good. But we surged upward, caught a heavy gust that kept us airborne just beyond the next swell. The Wasp radial engines roared and our speed picked up on the next contact. I got the hull up on step, and while the next wave hit us hard, it wasn't enough to put us back in a trough. *Tropic Angel* began to skip. She clipped the tops off the waves one after another until finally, despite all odds, she flew.

"Yeah!" Tyson shouted. "Let's fucking go!"

We were still in ground effect, skimming over the waves like a pelican, but we were in the air. As the airspeed increased, I allowed myself a look at the turbulent sky overhead. The clouds were low, overcast and riddled with lightning.

Out of the frying pan, into the fire.

But if we were going to take our chances with the wind or sea, every part of me preferred the sky.

I pulled back on the yoke and climbed, banking right and crosswind to the oncoming storm. Just then the dark shape of the Navajo screamed overhead, clearing the Mallard by mere feet across our bow.

I ducked as I swore and put *Tropic Angel* into a nosedive, nearly plunging back into the sea, but I pulled out of it five feet from the surface and came up again, fighting the wind to stay airborne while frantically searching the sky.

"What was that?" Whitney shouted from the cabin.

"Just hang on!"

Tyson was wide-eyed in the copilot seat, and I was sure I looked shaken myself, but if the captain of the ship is good for anything, they'd better keep their damned shit together.

I banked left, our wingtip nearly touching the waves, and scanned the overcast sky for the Navajo. I shouted to Tyson. "Find him on the iPad. See if his transponder is on."

Tyson scrambled to get the device on and paged to the map that showed traffic.

"I don't know if he's transmitting, but we are. You think that's how he sees us in this?"

The ceiling of clouds overhead was low, well under a thousand feet, maybe even six hundred. If Chuck was up in that and circling around for another pass at us, he had all the advantages while we were sitting ducks at this altitude.

But this duck wasn't made to sit.

"Shut off our transponder," I shouted. "He wants to find us in this soup, let him do it the hard way."

I pulled back on the yoke and climbed, soaring for the clouds.

It was a dangerous gamble, but no part of this was safe anyway.

We were nearly there when the left engine faltered, shuddering hard and flashing a light through the left window. Flames shot from the lower cowling and streaked aft behind the engine, a trail of oil and fuel possibly coming from the hole in the dead cylinder. The lowest cylinder had no compression, but that hadn't stopped the fuel from pouring through with every opening of the intake valve and exiting out the spark plug hole. Now all that unburned fuel was a hazard, leaking out of the cylinder, out the bottom of the engine, and into the cowling around it. With a loose ignition lead sparking around in there too, it had all the makings of a flying blowtorch.

We continued skyward with the left nacelle periodically lighting off like a Roman candle.

But I never made the clouds.

The Navajo came out of the layer above, descending like a hawk for a fish. I dove hard, down and left, nearly rolling over in a sixty degree bank and once again making my crew go weightless. We plummeted five hundred feet in seconds and once more had to skim the waves as the Navajo climbed back above us.

"That son of a bitch is determined, I'll give him that," I muttered.

Chuck's plane made a tight right turn, coming around hard on our tail.

The Mallard was a lot of things, but a fighter plane she was not.

Even so, I was determined to make every use of her power and brawn.

"Where do you think you can run to, boys?" a voice called out over the radio. I got the headset on my ears properly and recognized the voice as Chuck's coming over the UNICOM frequency.

"You're a sick bastard, Chuck," I said over the radio. "You're gonna kill yourself too with this stunt." I kept my head on a swivel to see if I could spot him.

"What's the matter, Angel? You can't take the tropical heat?"

"The truth's coming out about you one way or another, Chuck. No way you're getting out of this clean."

"Who you gonna tell when you're dead, chief?"

"I'll tell 'em right now," I said. I kept the plane headed toward the island, still skimming the surface at full power. "Hooper's Haven Traffic, anyone listening on frequency, Chuck Baum is responsible for the death of Dr. Julian Marcus and the pilot Harrison Taylor-Hardy. He killed them both in cold blood to cover up his history of murder in these islands. He's attempting to kill us right now."

I let off the mic switch and waited.

"You hear all that silence?" Chuck taunted. "Nobody is on frequency to listen to you whine. Nobody's gonna see you die, either. I could confess to killing a president out here and no one would give a shit. This is *my* island. You and Marcus and that flight instructor can curse me together from Hell."

"Chuck, you're even stupider than you look," I said back into the mic.

I glanced over to Tyson and he nodded, holding up the phone that he'd plugged into the headset's aux cord. "Got all of that."

"How many views will that one get in your reels?"

"A zillion. If we live."

The island raced toward us in the half-dark. We were doing nearly two hundred miles an hour, but the Navajo was faster and diving, so it was no doubt gaining on us. But I had one more trick up my sleeve.

"Got him on the iPad," Tyson said. "A hundred feet above, but shit, he's almost on top of us."

I pitched up, climbing fifty feet and narrowing the gap. I

banked left and craned my neck to see aft. The Navajo was even closer than I feared, bearing down hard. Chuck was trying to force us into the rising terrain of the island's bluffs ahead.

So I did what *Tropic Angel* was made for. I yanked the throttles back, idled the engines, and sank, plummeting back down to the surface of the ocean, flaring just before we hit, and letting the hull barely kiss the waves. The drag from the water arrested just enough of our momentum for the Navajo to overtake us high, barely clearing our engines as it too flared ahead of us to avoid hitting the water.

My throttles went back to full power and I pulled up hard, launching us back into the air in a climb that threatened to leave my guts in the seat of my pants, but we leveled out fifty feet above the Navajo's altitude. While Chuck wasted time looking for us in a right turn, I banked that way and cut him off, closing the gap at speed. He climbed too late and I nosed over, crushing his vertical stabilizer with my bow and smashing through his left propeller with my right wing pontoon. The impact was just enough to send the Navajo careening back toward the surface. The fuselage struck the water, skipped off it, and Chuck somehow kept it in the air, but too late. As I hauled back on the yoke and ascended over the rising island terrain, the Navajo barreled straight into the rocky bluffs ahead and exploded in a ball of fire.

THIRTY-SIX

CRASH

TROPIC ANGEL GRAZED the tops of the trees on the bluff as we cleared it. Wind off the sea tossed the plane around like a toy, threatening to smash us back to the earth at any moment in a downdraft, but my grip was steel on the controls. I wasn't going anywhere without a fight.

Despite still being airborne, we were yawing hard right. My right wing pontoon was in tatters and dragging in the wind.

"I need to put this thing on the ground!" I shouted to Tyson. "Get the gear down!"

He activated the landing gear handle and I reduced power to keep from ascending into the clouds. The ceiling was coming down on us fast and visibility was dropping with it. I couldn't make out the airfield and the left engine was smoking heavily again.

"There! I'm going to try to put us down on that." I pointed to a stretch of open space off our port side.

"We've only got two green," Tyson said, gesturing to the landing gear indicator. The main wheels had extended, but the nose gear hadn't come out. No doubt a casualty of our impact with the Navajo.

"We'll have to belly land the nose. I'll hold it off as long as I can."

I reduced power further and put out the first notch of flaps.

"That's Mali Solomon's golf course," Tyson said.

"Tonight it's an airport," I said and pulled power all the way back on the engines. I dumped full flaps and pitched for landing.

The wind was gusting so hard, I worried we might stall out over the trees before clearing them, but we dropped into the fairway of Mali's golf course with a low enough airspeed that when we touched down with the main wheels, the plane only made it a hundred feet before the hull at the bow made contact with the soft grass. I'd hauled back on the yoke as long as I could, but we were a plow now. On the bright side, I didn't have to use the brakes.

When the plane finally skidded to a full stop, I looked over at Tyson and found him just staring out the front windshield, his hands still gripping the seat's armrests. He gagged and put a hand to his mouth and choked back whatever had been threatening to come up.

"You good?" I asked, pulling my headset off my head and letting it fall to the floor.

"I'm good." He swallowed again for good measure. "But I think I might need a drink."

"You and I both, buddy."

I finished shutdown and unbuckled myself to check on our other passengers. Whitney was still in her seat, also vaguely green.

"This doesn't look much like Miami," she said with a wry glance out the window.

"Shoot. You noticed."

Her tone grew serious. "What happened to that other plane? We thought we saw an explosion."

I looked from her to Fabienne. "Chuck made an unscheduled landing. I don't think we'll be seeing him again."

"Good riddance." Fabienne unbuckled herself and stood. "Bastard deserved it. But it's like I'm cursed to never leave this damned island." The wind whistled around the fuselage and rocked the plane so much she had to hold onto the seat to keep her balance. "Where are we?"

"Mali Solomon's property."

"Oh, great. You couldn't think of a worse place to set down?"

"Really wanted to get a round of golf in before we left." I moved past the women toward the boarding door. "I'm going to check the condition of the plane. Stay here."

With the way the plane was rocking and swaying in the wind, no one looked in danger of rushing out after me.

I was met with a blast of air that blew my hair back when I opened the boarding door. The rain had lessened to a drizzle, but that was being flung sideways at high speed. Tree branches littered the golf course and palm fronds and leaves blew past like tumbleweeds. I was forced to squint as I put the ladder out and heaved a leg over the side. My shirt had dried to the wound in my back as I flew, but it ripped loose again as I climbed down the ladder. I winced as I made it under the left wing and around front to have a look at the engine that had been smoking.

The lower nacelle was discolored from heat and oil and some of the paint had blistered. But there was more mess than damage, with streaks of oil running aft and leaking out of skin sheets and joints in the wing. Overall the engine had handled the heat okay. Even with the nose gear collapsed, the engines sat high enough that the propellers hadn't touched the ground on the landing. The intermittent flames had extinguished themselves in the dives, so with a spark plug back in the lowest cylinder again, the engine might still run okay. Could have been a lot worse.

The hull was made of tough stuff. The bow structure would need inspecting after our contact with the Navajo's tail, and the nose landing gear would need repair, but *Tropic Angel* had come out of the contact as well as could be expected. Not many planes survived mid-air collisions.

Walking around to the right wing, I frowned at the one significant casualty. The plane's right wing pontoon had been smashed by Chuck's propeller and torn to bits. Thankfully the prop had only just hit the pontoon, missing the wing, so I had my fingers crossed that the wing spar itself was okay, but I'd need to fully replace the pontoon.

We were done flying for today, that much was clear.

There were lights in the trees, a building through the woods with windows aglow. The idea of a dry place to ride out the rest of this storm wasn't the worst thing I could think of, so I trudged back around the Mallard and back up the boarding ladder to address my passengers.

"There's a house nearby. I say we walk."

I took Fabienne's satchel from her and slung it gingerly over one shoulder, then helped the women down the ladder.

Whitney's glasses were flecked with raindrops as she looked around. "This isn't the same part of the golf course we were on before."

"We might be farther south," I said.

A wooden bridge beyond a sand trap showed where a walking path entered the woods. I took a couple of flashlights from the plane and we navigated our way to it, shielding our eyes from the wind.

Branches were still coming down from trees in the gusting wind, so we ran the short distance down the path toward the lit windows, emerging into a yard I now recognized. The garden was worse for wear, several trellises blown over and plants uprooted, but we were in the back acreage of Ruth Solomon's home. To my surprise, the rear door of the house opened at our approach and Ruth herself stood silhouetted in the light. After the day we'd had, I half expected her to be holding a gun.

Her intense stare was focused beyond me, however, and I turned to find it was Fabienne who had her attention.

"I knew one day someone would come," Ruth said.

Rain ran down Fabienne's face, the light from the interior glistening on her cheeks. With Ruth backlit from the house, her face was in shadow, and for a moment I was caught by the strange reflection they made of each other, youth and age, vengeance and . . . what? Pain?

The older woman beckoned Fabienne inside, and once Fabienne was through the door, Ruth turned to the rest of us.

"You've made it this far," she shouted through the wind. "Might as well come in."

So we did.

THIRTY-SEVEN

IMPACT

THE INSIDE of Ruth Solomon's cottage was warm, the humid storm air having wicked its way indoors to thicken the atmosphere. The lights were bright but flickered occasionally as power lines on the island struggled in the wind.

Ruth Solomon emerged from a hallway with an armload of towels and handed them out solemnly in a communion line ending with me. She took in my bloodied state without comment and gave me the last towel before moving to the sitting room.

She lived alone as best I could tell, the cottage kept immaculately clean. The sitting room was furnished in a style that would make for great photographs in a magazine spread but offered questionable comfort. The others dried off and took seats, but the light-colored furniture looked expensive so I stayed standing, preferring to bleed alone in the background.

I wasn't the focus of this conversation anyway. Fabienne and Ruth had barely taken their eyes off each other since our arrival. Whitney sat close at Fabienne's side, a vigilant wingwoman, weapons hot. My duel with Chuck on the runway had been tense, but there was another kind of tension simmering here, something innately feminine and beyond my ken—three women, each of a perilous kind of beauty, on a collision course. Even Tyson sat quietly reserved in the face of it, watching.

Fabienne finally spoke, somehow by right.

"This all has to do with you. Not Mali. Doesn't it."

Ruth Solomon was perched straight-backed on the edge of her armchair, ankles and wrists crossed. She regarded the younger woman calmly. "You and my daughter are nearly the same age. You might have had similar lives had things not gone the way they did."

My eyes drifted to the mantel over the fireplace. The framed photographs were all of Mali. Except one. At the far left edge was the photograph I recognized from Julian Marcus's house. The four teens, arms draped over one another's shoulders. A smiling, beautiful Ruth, with Julian and Edwin at each of her sides, Jacqui standing apart.

"It's not easy being a mother," Ruth continued. "You are asked to make choices. Sometimes choices you never could have imagined. It's a duty you take on, and it requires sacrifices for the sake of your children."

"Does your daughter know what you've done?" Whitney asked.

Ruth shook her head, almost imperceptibly. "It is not a mother's job to burden her children. We're the bow. They are the arrows. And she's flown faster and farther than us all, hasn't she? Thanks to me."

"You were sick," Whitney said. "Was that why you came back to the island? Or was it something else?"

"A man, you mean? Did I come running back from my failed marriage? That's what most of the island thought. A young child. No more husband. Had to flee home. One can't blame them for assuming, I suppose." Ruth lifted her chin. "But they didn't offer to help much either way, did they? Wanted to see me on my knees, most of them. Julian was the only one I could rely on. And dear Edwin, of course. They understood a mother's duty to her child."

"My father was not a sacrifice." Fabienne spoke so quietly, I found myself leaning in to hear.

Ruth turned and watched her the way someone might watch a wounded animal struggling to move. Except Ruth's eyes failed to show pity.

"I don't know anything about your father. He came much later. One of Chuck's other finds. It was someone else who sacrificed for me. The first donor."

"Victim, you mean," Fabienne's voice was stronger this time. "Sacrifices are offered, not taken."

"We all sacrificed something," Ruth said.

The women stared at each other, unwavering.

A phone rang on a countertop behind me. A landline. I reached for it.

"Leave it," Ruth said.

My hand hovered over the ringing phone, but then I pulled it back.

"My daughter desperately wants me up in the house with her," Ruth said. "Because of the storm."

The ringing stopped.

"It's going to come out," Whitney said. "The deaths. The victims. Julian Marcus's addictions. His willingness to transplant stolen organs for profit. Chuck and his trafficking operation. All of it. And it will all come back to you. And Mali. She'll be exposed. What good will all of these sacrifices be then?"

"Mali is blameless," Ruth said with force. "And Chuck was blackmailing Julian for years, keeping him in it. Forcing the poor man to continue."

"I suppose you hold yourself blameless too," I interjected.

"Even though Dr. Marcus had gotten clean and had a real chance to escape this island."

"I cared deeply for Julian," she retorted. "I've always been concerned for his health and state of mind."

"So concerned, you called Chuck at sea and let him know Dr. Marcus was leaving? We saw Marcus here at your house that day. He loved you too much to leave without saying goodbye, is that it?"

"I've always loved Julian," she fired back. "For forty years I've been his closest confidant. Not that it matters now. Poor Julian is dead."

"And Chuck. And Edwin," I said.

Ruth looked shocked for the first time. "Edwin? You killed my Edwin, too?" When I didn't reply, she only nodded. "I knew when I first saw you and heard your name—*Luke Angel*. I knew that you'd only be an angel of death for us."

"There's competition for that title on this island," I replied.

"Yes, there is," Fabienne said, standing. As she did so, she pulled the 0.22 pistol from behind her back and leveled it at Ruth.

"Whoa, shit," Tyson blurted, getting to his feet.

"Fabienne," Whitney said, also rising slowly. "Honey, think this through."

"She has thought it through," Ruth said. She rose as well. "Haven't you?"

The two women continued their staring contest across from each other. Fabienne's jaw clenched. The gun didn't waver.

Ruth took a step forward and Fabienne did also. When the two women were only an arm's length apart, Ruth moved forward the final inch so that the barrel of the gun was pressed to her forehead, directly between her eyes.

Outside, headlights swept down the drive and illuminated the front of the cottage.

"The storm is finally at an end," Ruth said, and closed her eyes.

Fabienne's arm started to shake. Then she screamed and pulled the trigger.

I flinched.

The gun clicked on the empty chamber.

Ruth's eyes reopened slowly.

Fabienne pressed the muzzle to Ruth's forehead a second longer and hissed at her. "Your storm is just beginning."

The door to the cottage flew open and Mali Solomon stood in the doorway, the wind blowing in with her. Her eyes went wide.

Fabienne lowered her weapon and turned to face her. Then she dropped her gun to the floor.

THIRTY-EIGHT

RECOVERY

I STEPPED out of the lobby elevator at the Solomon Center just after dawn with seven stitches in my back. The mood upstairs had been somber but professional. The staff even gave me a clean, donated T-shirt to wear out of the building. It said "Coconut Chuck's Boneyard Bar and Grill" on it.

The storm had passed. Cell service had been restored to the island around 3 a.m., but I decided I'd wait till daylight to call Reese.

Deputy Thorpe met me in the lobby. I imagined she was as tired as I was.

"Taken a lot of statements tonight," she said. "But I imagine yours might require the most follow up."

"Don't hold it against me if I don't love the idea of sticking around this island much longer."

She rested a hand on her hip. "Half dozen detectives from Nassau will be landing here in an hour. You'd better believe they'll be looking at me hard too when they show up. I'll probably be on immediate probation till they figure out what to do about the constable's post."

"You found Swain?"

"I sent the EMTs down to check him. Cordoned off the area. But I'll leave the evidence collecting to the homicide detectives. They insisted."

"Did you have any idea Swain was in on this organ trafficking scheme with Chuck and Dr. Marcus?"

"The *alleged* organ trafficking scheme." She gave me a cautious appraisal. "But between you and me, I had my suspicions he was into something, at least with Vaughn and his crew. Seems those boys always found the right way to weasel out of their convictions. And their lawyer wasn't nearly good enough to explain it."

"Where is Vaughn? Do I need to worry about him popping out of the bushes at me on my way out of here?"

She adjusted her gun belt. "Someone from Pelican Roost actually called in a report this morning on Vaughn. Seems he filled up his lobster boat a couple hours ago and failed to pay for the fuel. Took off south in a hurry. Didn't make it far though. Ran into one of our interceptors that was making its way here from Sandy Point. Don't know if you've seen any of our new interceptors, but you don't run from them. He's in custody for the moment while we sort this mess out."

"And Ruth Solomon?"

"At the station. She voluntarily confessed to accepting a trafficked organ in a transplant, but that's already more than her lawyer wanted her to say. I'll have to let homicide deal with the rest and decide what other charges she'll draw for Dr. Marcus's death. It's going to make quite the scandal."

"You mind if I make a few calls? I've got a plane to fix."

"Just so long as you don't wander far."

"Don't worry," I said. "It's a small island."

"About damned time," Reese said when she picked up.

"Worried about me?" The sun was barely highlighting the horizon, but Reese sounded like she'd been awake awhile.

"Your dog was worried. He won't eat. As you know, he's my main priority."

"As he should be."

"You good?"

I studied the brightening sky and the wispy post-storm clouds that were turning a pale orange. "Yeah. I think so. But I'm going to have you ask a favor from a friend."

"You have more than one friend?"

"There's a Mallard based over in Fort Pierce. I'm hoping they'll let you borrow their right wing pontoon for a few days on your way over here to help me ferry *Tropic Angel* home."

"What did you do?"

"I'll send you a parts list. See if you can put the story together from that. Five bucks says you can't."

"Tyson okay?"

Lights were on in the village bakery, so I began walking that way. "Honestly, I think this might have been a fairly formative trip for him."

"Guy stuff?"

"I'll let him tell you," I said, then thought about it. "Even better, you should subscribe to his reels."

Whitney was still asleep when I got back to her motel room. I set a fresh croissant and a cup of coffee on her nightstand, but when she didn't stir, I brushed her hair from her face with a fingertip and headed back out. Tyson was likewise asleep, but I spotted Fabienne on a deck chair overlooking the water at the back of the motel. She was staring off into the morning sun with her arms draped in her lap.

When I made it down to her, I offered Fabienne one of the other coffees I'd picked up from the bakery and she accepted. "Mind if I join you? Looks like a good thinking spot."

"It's what I needed."

I settled into a deck chair beside her and waited.

"I'm not sure what I'm going to do now," she said, cupping her coffee with both hands.

"You feel like you have any closure?"

"Not really. We found my dad's killer, but it didn't bring him back. I'm still furious with everything about this situation, and I'm also just . . . tired."

"I'm not a dad, but if I was yours, I think I'd be really proud of what you've accomplished. You brought some justice to a situation that no one else could. If it wasn't for you, who knows how long Chuck and Julian Marcus could have been operating in these islands unnoticed."

"It's just a drop in the bucket, though. Do you know how many other ways my island gets exploited? Maybe it won't be illegal organ trafficking now, but there's always corruption in Haiti. The gangs, the drugs, the kidnappings. When I think about the life my dad lived back home, the one he got me out of, and how much he sacrificed to see me succeed, what good did it do him? I dropped out of nursing school to do this. To see him avenged. I just don't see how I go back to my life after this. Pretend it didn't happen? Go back to Haiti? Try to change things?"

"You're too close to it now. That makes it hard to see your way forward. Happens to all of us. But when the weather's shit and you can't see any kind of destination, you just keep climbing. You already succeeded at something more difficult than most people will face in their lifetimes. You're what? Early twenties?

Not to sound like an old man, but this is barely the first leg of your journey. You just need to get a little more altitude. Once the clouds clear, I bet you'll see the rest of your way on just fine."

She studied me over the lid of her coffee cup. "Can you turn anything into a flying analogy?"

"Always. Because attitudes in life and attitudes in flying are the same thing. It's easy. You just keep the blue side up."

She smiled. "You really should be a dad. You've already got the cheesy material."

"Maybe I will be one day." I shrugged and sipped my coffee. "But let's hope it's not on this island."

THIRTY-NINE
BARFLIES

IT TOOK three days to get the Mallard back to the airfield and in a condition to fly home. It involved us securing the bow onto a flatbed truck to get the nose gear doors straightened, then backing the plane into the water to motor it around the island. A couple of gear extension and retraction tests in the cove went smoothly, so I was able to get the big bird airborne from the water and land it back on the airfield for additional repairs. The process was aided greatly by the arrival of Reese with the borrowed wing pontoon, but delayed by the arrival of the detectives from Nassau.

Fortunately, the lead detective who took my statements knew her job, and thanks to Tyson's timely recording of Chuck's threats on the radio, we had some decent evidence to back up our seemingly far-fetched story. Whitney's account corroborated mine as well, and Chuck's bunker was gone through and cataloged. I wasn't privy to the evidence in the case, but got the impression they'd found more than enough there to suggest he'd been in the organ and drug trafficking business for decades.

Chuck's surveillance videos also showed his abduction of Tyson and most of the hangar shootout.

The biggest aid to the case ended up being some of Vaughn's crew. With him in custody for his involvement, stories started coming out of the woodwork from Pelican Roost, largely from those fed up with the scourge of drugs in the town. The finger pointing caused Vaughn himself to get vocal. He assigned blame to Coconut Chuck, Edwin Swain, and anyone else he could in an attempt to save himself.

Whitney's story broke in the Herald while she was still on the island. I read it on my phone with a margarita at the local dive bar Katie had started working at. This place had less tourist flair than The Boneyard, but plenty of local color. A few salty residents of the bar actually applauded when Whitney walked in the door to meet me, though that may have been what they did for all beautiful women who graced the place.

"You did a nice job," I said, pulling out the barstool beside me for her to sit on. She was mostly covered up again, back to tropical librarian mode in her attire, with another long flowy skirt to her ankles. But her top might have loosened a few buttons on my behalf. Sexy librarian.

"It's the tip of the iceberg, obviously, but it gets the story out," she said.

"You didn't rip into Mali Solomon like I expected."

"I don't only write merciless takedowns of celebrities. There is more to my journalistic style than that."

"I'm aware. I was just curious how your feelings about her might have changed. Seemed like you took a new view."

Whitney sighed. "I think the rich will continue to throw money at problems the way they always have, if that's what you mean. So situations like Haiti, and the victimization of other impoverished places will continue. But I don't know if I necessarily see Mali as a face of that anymore. I drove by one of the storm clean-up sites on my way here and spotted her on the side of the road just helping pick up debris."

"No camera crew documenting it for social media attention?"

"None that I saw. I think the girl was just trying to do something to help her island. I know Ruth Solomon did a criminal thing to ensure the life she had, but in the end, her daughter did turn out all right."

"Kid's got a good heart. Maybe she should be famous for that. You stop and talk to her?"

"I did. And you know what she said? She offered to give me a ride back to Miami in her plane and do an exclusive interview on the way."

"Wow. You going to take her up on it?"

"I think I might. I got the impression she's going to do the one interview with me, then clam up. This place is turning into a media frenzy. You see all the new arrivals today?"

"Heard the planes."

"I think every reporter on the East Coast is finding a way here. They dubbed it 'Murder Island' in the Times today. I had ten emails this morning requesting interviews with me as one of the 'killer's surviving victims.' I'm sure if anyone could find your email, you'd have just as many."

"Good thing I'm hiding here then." I sipped my margarita, then rested a hand on her knee. "Sorry to be losing a passenger for the flight home though. We've been through a lot together."

She nodded gravely and fixed me with her sparkling blue eyes. "While I can't say this is exactly how I'd like to spend my next island work trip, there have been perks."

I reached under her barstool and took a firm grip under the seat, then dragged it closer till our knees were touching. Whitney leaned into me and draped her arms around my neck. "I think I could postpone the flight home until tomorrow morning, though, if you have a few perks left in you."

I put a hand to the side of her face and caressed her cheek with my thumb. "Well, I'm nothing if not perky." She smiled, then I pulled her the rest of the way to me and kissed her.

The locals at the bar cheered again.

FORTY

HOMEWARD BOUND

TYSON CLIMBED through the keyhole-shaped entryway to the flight deck of *Tropic Angel* and took a seat beside me for the ride home. He'd found some more new clothes at the store we'd previously visited and was now sporting a bright shirt in Bahamian flag colors. He had his shades on and had stuck his headset on the top of his head like the crown of a Roman emperor.

"You want to do the takeoff this morning?" I asked.

"For real?"

"I think you've earned it on this trip."

"Hell yes. Yes, I did."

We had the plane back in the cove after testing the final patches to the hull. The interior had stayed nice and dry this time, which was no doubt a comfort to the passengers. Basil waved from the jon boat after freeing us from the buoy. The turquoise water of the cove was calm and the tide was already easing us out.

Fabienne was in the nearest seat to the front on the starboard side, and she gave me a thumbs up when I leaned around the bulkhead to check on her. Reese had already flown home, but we'd added a couple more passengers to the manifest, a father and daughter whose house had been damaged in the storm and were headed to Tampa to stay with family.

Fabienne wore an expression I hadn't seen on her before as she conversed with the father and daughter across from her. Looked a lot like some peace. But she mouthed a question to me.

"What's that? I said, pushing one earphone away to hear her better.

"Is the heater off?"

I gave her a thumbs up. "All good."

"Thanks."

I double-checked it just to be sure.

"Landing gear is up and locked for takeoff," Tyson said in my ear. He had the checklist in hand and was going through items. "Trim's set."

I slid my headset back onto my ears. "Doors are closed, tail stand is stowed. Mooring lines free."

We worked through the engine start checklist as a team and soon had the big radials rumbling smoothly on either side. Out the window, Mali Solomon's Embraer Phenom 300 taxied toward the end of Runway 9. Whitney was on board somewhere and Mali herself was in the pilot's seat, another pilot from her all-female crew in the flight deck with her. I rolled down my pilot-side window, stuck an arm out, and waved.

Whoever designed the Phenom hadn't factored in a need for window cranks, so Mali was obligated to keep all her limbs inside, but she waved nonetheless. The high pitch of the turbines carried over the water and mingled with the deep thrumming of the Mallard's radials. I rolled the window back up and turned my attention to Tyson again. He was nearly done with the pre-takeoff list. He double-checked the radio frequencies and then put his hand up to the throttles. "You ready for this?"

"Hold on, you don't have your phone in the camera mount yet. You aren't going to record this one for your reels?"

He turned and regarded the empty phone mount, but then focused his eyes ahead. "Nah. Somehow, I don't think it'll ever live up to the real thing anyway. Plus, I kinda want to do this one just for me."

He grinned his bright smile at me and I nodded.

"Bet."

His mouth dropped open in shock. "Hey, you actually used that right."

"'Cause I'm a bussin' dude with a dank ride."

"Nah. Now you ruined it. You're back to bein' old."

I shrugged. "Room for improvement."

"Yeah. Me too." He pushed forward on the throttles till the manifold pressures hit their targets. I followed along. *Tropic Angel* responded with enthusiasm. The big plane plowed forward and climbed up on step easily in the calm water. Plumes of spray arched up from the keel in a rooster tail of prismatic color and then lessened as the plane leveled out. We skipped along the surface giving one last kiss to the now emerald Caribbean sea, and then Tyson pulled back on the yoke and we soared upward.

The view of crystalline water expanded beneath us and the few scattered white clouds on the distant horizon beckoned. Engine parameters all looked good, and Tyson's grin settled into a smile of satisfaction. "Damn that was tight. All right. Your airplane, Cap."

"Nice work." I rested my hand back on the yoke. "My airplane."

Tyson stretched an arm along the windowsill and took in the view. "Yeah, man. This is Heaven."

And I agreed. We flew on into the sun-drenched sky.

I kept the blue side up.

Thanks for reading.

If you enjoyed this book and would like more, **please leave it a review**! You can also follow Nate Van Coops on Amazon or Goodreads to be notified of future books.

Want to read a fantastic **original opening scene** to this book that I struggled to cut? You do. You should. Here is a link to the exclusive bonus content where you get it. Enjoy.

https://dl.bookfunnel.com/cduig873yi

ACKNOWLEDGMENTS

Something I hear often from readers upon publishing a book is: "That was great. Where's the next one!"

I wish I could write as fast as you read. But thanks for sticking with me book after book, reading my newsletters, writing reviews, sending me emails, and reading my next book, year after year.

I have some readers now that I've heard from repeatedly for the last ten years of writing and that thrills me to no end.

I feel very fortunate to be able to do this job. I owe you one, so I'm already working hard on the next book for you.

Thanks also to my beta team, the TYPE PROS, who took this book up around the airfield first to make sure it wouldn't crash and burn. Your enthusiasm for the story and willingness to pause other activities and even give your kids more screen-time so you could finish this book, gave me the confidence to know it would fly.

Specific thanks this round to: Marilyn Bourdeau, Julie DeStefano, Mark Hale, Maarja Kruusmets, Judy Eiler, Eric Lizotte, Ken Robbins, Claire Manger, Yvonne Mitchell, Steve Kent, Ginelle Blanch, Elaine Davis, Sarah Van Coops-Bush, Steve Bryant, and Bethany Cousins.

Nick, Jay, Alex, Michael, and Bill, thanks for being great guys to hang around the kava shop with and pretend we have hard jobs. You make the day-to-day a lot of fun. Thanks also to Casey, Cassidy, Kate, Julian and all the other staff at Driftwood for accommodating and caffeinating this writer.

And to my writer friends, Lucy Score, Alan Lee, Cecelia Mecca, James Blatch, Boo Walker, and T. Ellery Hodges. You are a daily inspiration. Also a big thanks to the Tropical Authors group. Excited to officially be among your ranks!

My wife and kids: You never read these acknowledgments, but one day you might. I love you. I'll squeeze you when I see you.

ABOUT THE AUTHOR

NATE VAN COOPS is a commercial pilot, designated mechanic examiner, and certified flight instructor in St. Petersburg Florida. His addictions to tacos and pickleball wage a war for supremacy daily. When not writing, or flying at his favorite airport, you'll find him e-biking around St. Pete with his wife and kids. He also writes science fiction books under the name Nathan Van Coops. Learn more at natevancoops.com.

To say hello, or to inquire about the availability of film or television rights, send email to: nathan@nathanvancoops.com